OUSHATA MASSACRE

ARROW AND SABER BOOK 1

ROBERT VAUGHAN

Oushata Massacre
Arrow and Saber Book I

Robert Vaughan

Paperback Edition
Copyright © 2018 (as revised) Robert Vaughan

Wolfpack Publishing
6032 Wheat Penny Ave
Las Vegas, NV 89122

This book is a work of fiction. Any references to historical events, real people or real places are used fictitiously. Other names, characters, places and events are products of the author's imagination, and any resemblance to actual events, places or persons, living or dead, is entirely coincidental.

All rights reserved. No part of this book may be reproduced by any means without the prior written consent of the publisher, other than brief quotes for reviews.

Paperback ISBN: 978-1-64119-388-7
Ebook ISBN: 978-1-64119-387-0

Library of Congress Control Number: 2018957884

OUSHATA MASSACRE

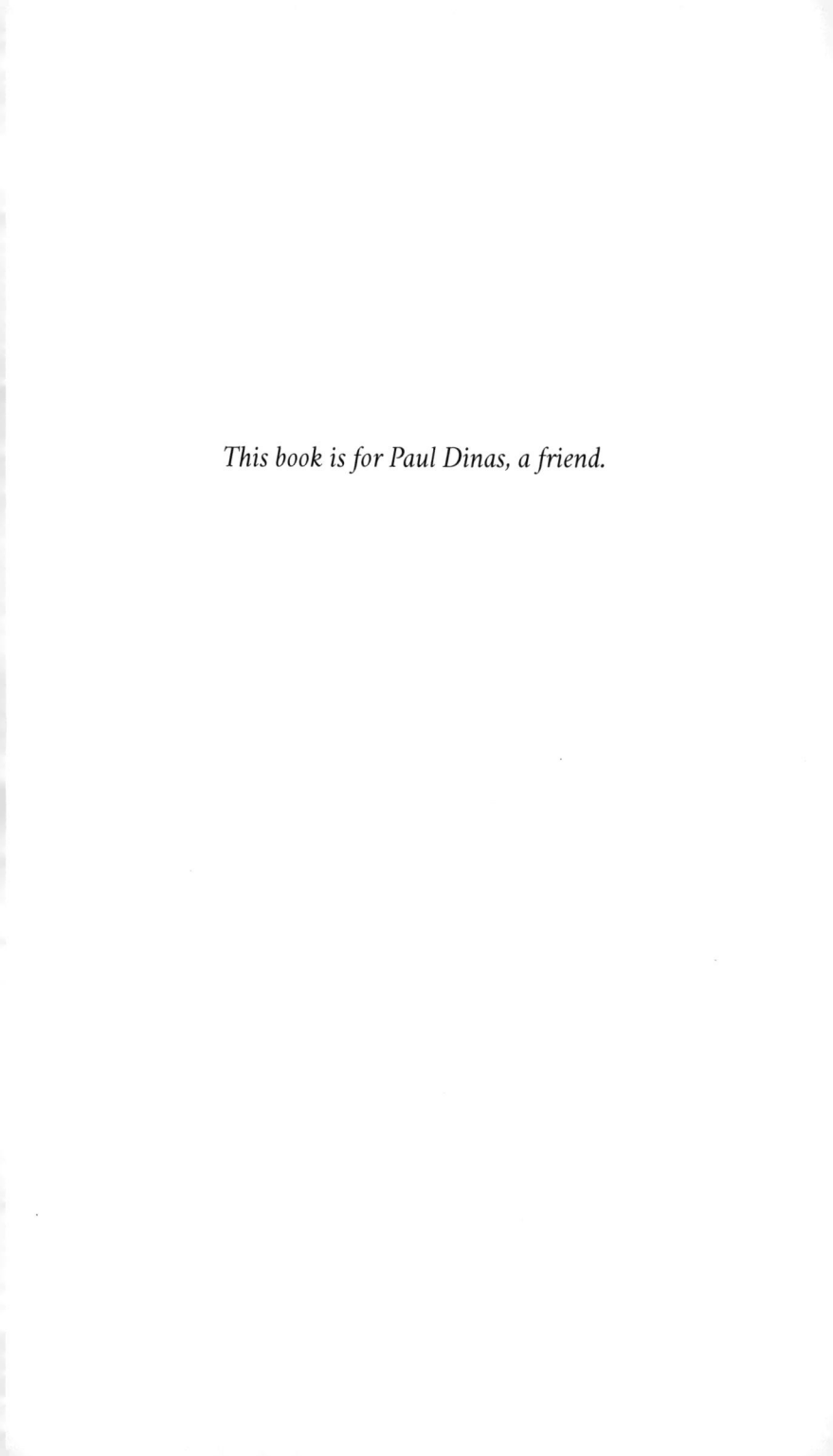

This book is for Paul Dinas, a friend.

OUSHATA MASSACRE

1

With his bag packed, Second Lieutenant Marcus Cavanaugh crossed the quadrangle where the regiment was hurrying to get into position for the reveille formation, walking carefully through the dust and the horse droppings to keep from dirtying the shine of his boots. He was twenty-one years old, just over six feet tall, with broad shoulders, vivid blue eyes, and brown hair. Three months earlier, in June of 1868, he had stood on the plains at West Point to receive his degree and his Army commission. Now, he was standing in the sally port of the east wall of Fort Reynolds, Colorado, watching the machinations of what had already become his life. He had no father or mother, or other family ties.

Across the quadrangle, the door to the headquarters building opened and the post commander stepped outside, mounted the horse being held by his orderly, then rode to the flagpole at the edge of the parade ground. It wasn't necessary, Marcus knew, for Colonel Pettibone to personally take command of the reveille formation. He could have delegated that job to his second-in-command, Major Conklin, or to the next higher rank, Captain Forsyth. But Colonel Pettibone enjoyed it, and he turned what should have been a routine morning formation into an event of pomp and ceremony.

Commands and supplementary commands rippled through the ranks as the regiment came to attention. Sabers flashed in the early-morning sun as platoon leaders, then company commanders, and finally battalion commanders rendered their reports to Major Conklin. The executive officer received the reports, then turned toward Colonel Pettibone and brought his saber up in a smart chin salute.

"Fourth Cavalry Regiment all present and accounted for, sir!" he barked.

Pettibone returned the salute, then sat astride his horse for a moment, looking out over his command. Most Cavalry units, when in-garrison, held dismounted drill for the reveille formation, not going to the bother of saddling the horses. Colonel Pettibone was different. He insisted that the men not only be mounted, but in the proper uniform. That meant shell jackets for the troopers, and blue frock coats for officers. The only concession to the locale was the fact that Pettibone did not insist that his command wear the hated kepi. Instead, officers and enlisted wore the so-called Jeff Davis hat, a brim hat pinned up on the right side and dressed in front with crossed sabers over the number 4, indicating that they were members of the 4th Cavalry Regiment.

Lieutenant Colonel Pettibone was Marcus's first commander, and as Pettibone himself was quick to point out, he was not like any other he'd encounter in the western territories.

"I was a major general during the war," Pettibone had said to Marcus when the young lieutenant reported in. Pettibone wore his red-gold hair shoulder length, and his whiskers were trimmed into a Vandyke beard. "Before that insolent pup, Custer, was promoted to major general, he was in my command. Now he is getting all the glory. Well, by thunder, he'll not recover his stars before I do. The only place left for a soldier to make his mark in this army is out here, fighting the savages. And I shall do just that, sir. You may depend upon it, I shall do just that."

Pettibone dismissed the formation, then rode across the quadrangle toward Marcus and dismounted. He turned his horse over to an orderly with instructions that it be unsaddled and returned to the stable. Marcus came to attention and saluted his commander. He had been given the privilege of missing the morning formation because he was about to leave on a special assignment and was, even now, waiting for the stage.

"Well, Lieutenant, all ready to go, I see?" "Yes, sir," Marcus replied.

"Pity I couldn't provide you with an ambulance and a proper military escort to Cheyenne Wells, but with the wheel broken on one of the ambulances, we've only one left." "That's quite all right, sir," Marcus answered. "The stage will be here shortly."

"You have everything you need? Orders, travel vouchers for the men?"

"Yes, sir. I have everything."

"This is quite a responsibility for a second lieutenant, you know. You are to return to New York to pick up a platoon of new recruits and escort them back to Fort Reynolds. And not only that, I shall also charge you with the duty of turning them into soldiers. But as you only arrived here from West Point a short time ago, you are still well schooled in the art of drill and should do well."

"I will do my best, sir," Marcus said. Though he wouldn't speak of it, secretly he was disappointed that he was going to have to return to the East so soon after arriving out here. There had been several skirmishes with the Cheyenne lately. As yet he had not been involved in any of them, and he was afraid he would miss the opportunity if he left.

"Lieutenant!" a guard called down from the top of the wall. "The stage is a-comin'."

"Thank you, McKay," Marcus replied.

Shortly thereafter Marcus could hear the crack of the stage driver's whip and his loud whistle as the coach drew near. A nearby private picked up Marcus's bag without being asked, then stepped through the sally port to the outside of the post and flagged down the stage. The shotgun guard crawled down and opened the leather flap over the boot for the suitcase, while Marcus, with a good-bye salute, climbed into the coach. There were three passengers inside, all men. As they identified themselves, Marcus learned that one was a leather-goods salesman, one a farmer, and the third, a lawyer.

It was a long, tiring ride, though the monotony was relieved somewhat by a lapboard and a deck of cards the salesman had brought with him. The drummer traveled often by stage and had learned that a little diversion made the trips a bit easier.

It was about noon when, from atop the stage, the driver blew a loud bleat on his horn. He blew it a second time, then a third, before the salesman got a strange expression on his face, then stretched around to look out the window.

"That's funny," he said. "We've saluted three times but old John Minner hasn't answered." When he saw that the other passengers hadn't yet understood the significance of it, he went on, rather enjoying his role of seasoned traveler.

"You see," he explained, "the driver gives a long bleat on his horn to let the man at the stage depot know we're comin'. Then the depot men . . . this here is Minner's Switch, named after John Minner . . . well, John gives a toot back to let the driver know he heard. Then John starts roundin' up the horses so that by the time we get there, he has a fresh team ready to be harnessed. Only, John ain't tooted back."

Up top, the driver shouted to his team and hauled

back on the reins, while putting his foot on the brake, bringing the coach to a stop.

"Iffen you fellas want to get out and stretch your legs a mite, go ahead," the driver called down.

The four men stepped out of the coach. Three promptly began relieving themselves, while Marcus walked toward the driver and shotgun guard, who were standing together at the head of the team in a quiet conference.

"Anything wrong?" Marcus asked.

The driver spit out a wad of chewing tobacco, then wiped his mouth with the back of his hand before he answered.

"Well, now, maybe they is, an' maybe they ain't," he said. "Lookin' over in that direction, I don't see no smoke or nothin'. But I ain't gettin' no answer to my horn, either."

"Has he ever failed to answer before?" Marcus asked. "I mean, is it possible that he could be . . . indisposed?"

The driver looked at Marcus. "Is that a fancy word for bein' drunk?"

"Could be," Marcus admitted.

The driver shook his head. "Some of the other fellas, maybe. But ol' John, he's a teetotaler. Don't reckon I've ever seen him touch a drop. He ain't drunk, soljer boy. He just ain't answerin'."

"You pretty good with a long gun?" the guard asked.

"Yes," Marcus said. This was no time for false

modesty, and he had taken the top award for marksmanship in his class.

"Besides the shotgun I'm carryin', I got two Henrys up in the boot. I'd be obliged iffen you'd take one of 'em an' come up on top 'til we get into the station."

"Of course," Marcus answered.

Fifteen minutes later, with Marcus on the roof of the stage, his rifle at the ready, the coach pulled into the depot.

The first thing they saw was another stagecoach. This had been the westbound coach, but there was no team attached, and the coach was tipped over on its side. A short distance away from the coach, a man lay sprawled on his stomach with the top of his head missing.

"That there is John Minner," the driver said, pointing to the body as he halted the team.

The driver, shotgun guard, and passengers got out of the coach gingerly, then began looking around the station, straining their eyes to see into the shadows and behind the corners. It was quiet . . . and dead still. When the windmill, answering a breeze, suddenly swung around with a loud squeak and clank and started spinning, Marcus and the others were startled. He swung his rifle toward the stable, only to see the windmill whirling into life.

"Billy, have you noticed that they ain't horse one in that stable," the guard said to the driver.

"Yep," the driver said. "I noticed that."

"Oh, my God!" the drummer suddenly shouted. He

turned and ran several steps, then started throwing up. Marcus looked over to see what had set him off, then he had to fight his own stomach. Behind the corner of the porch he saw two naked bodies ... a woman and a little girl. The little girl had been scalped; the woman, probably the little girl's mother, had not only been scalped, but had had her breasts cut off.

There were three more bodies inside. All three were men, and all had been scalped and had their gentials removed. Billy identified two of them as the driver and guard of the other stage. He didn't know the third man, but figured he may have been the husband and father to the woman and girl outside.

"What'll we do now, Lieutenant?" Billy asked.

Marcus was a little surprised that he had been asked by the stagecoach driver. But he was the Army, and he could understand how, in Billy's eyes, this had become an Army problem.

"How far to Cheyenne Wells?"

"With a fresh team, four hours," Billy answered. "With what we got ... I'd say six, maybe eight hours."

"If we get going right away, we could make it just after nightfall?",

"That's what I figure."

"All right," Marcus said. "Let's bury these people and get to Cheyenne Wells. From there, we can send a wire back to Fort Reynolds, and Colonel Pettibone can deal with whoever did this."

"What if they're still out there, waitin' for us?" the driver asked.

"Then we'll just have to fight our way through," Marcus said.

With a tired team, the driver had to stop twice as often to give the horses a breather. They had been gone from Minner's Switch for the better part of three hours. It was midafternoon and the sun seemed to hang halfway through its western arc, pouring down a blistering heat. Marcus was still riding on top of the stage, and he removed his hat and mopped at his face with his bandanna, then put the hat back on.

"Want a drink of water, Lieutenant?" the driver offered, passing his canteen back to Marcus.

"Thanks," Marcus said. He took a swallow, then handed the canteen back. A dry, rattling wind lifted dust from the plains. A dust cloud swirled high on the hot, rising air and spread a red halo around the sun. Even the sky had lost its soft blue to a dingy orange. So far Marcus had known only the summer heat of the plains, but the other men at the fort were quick to point out that it was even worse in the winter, when a heavy snowstorm would set in, causing the cattle, buffalo, and deer to huddle helplessly in fields of white, to starve and freeze to death.

And yet, despite the extremes of weather, there was a steady and ever-increasing immigration of white settlers. And with the coming of the railroad, the settlement would be even faster. The Indians realized it, too, and that was why they were making a last-ditch effort to drive the whites out.

"Lieutenant, I don't know if you see 'em or not," the

driver said, interrupting Marcus's thoughts. "But we got company."

"Where?"

"Off to our right, 'bout a hunnert fifty, maybe two hunnert yards. They been ridin' just on the other side of that ridgeline there."

Marcus looked in the direction indicated by the driver, then saw them. More accurately, he saw one of them slipping in behind a dump of rocks. He was angry with himself for not having seen them before the driver did. "Damn, I should've noticed," he said.

"Don't be down on yourself, Lieutenant. I been drivin' through here so much I don't have to see 'em. I got a feel for 'em."

"You men ready?"

"I got a shotgun and a rifle handy," the guard said.

"In the coach," Marcus called down. "There are Indians about two hundred yards off to the right. Have your weapons ready."

"I'm not armed," the lawyer called up. "Here," the guard said, handing his shotgun to Marcus. "Give 'im this. I'll take the other rifle for myself, and he don't have to be much of a shot to hit anything with this. I've got 'er loaded with double-aught buck." Marcus passed the shotgun and a little sack of shells down through the window to the lawyer, then he lay flat on the roof, cocked his rifle, and waited.

The Indians trailed alongside for about half an hour longer, then, as the coach approached a ford in a creek, the driver turned toward Marcus. "They'll have to do somethin' now. On the other side of this here ford the land is flat for more'n a mile to either side. They'll have to show themselves."

Marcus waited, every nerve ending in his body tense. He had been looking forward to his first engagement with the Cheyenne, but he had not imagined it this way. He had thought he would be at the head of his troops, surrounded by well-armed, well-trained men. He was the only soldier on a stagecoach of five civilians. Hardly the classic battle to begin his fighting career.

The coach rolled through the ford, kicking up sand and bubbles of water. When it came out on the other side, the Cheyenne war party made their first attack. There were at least a dozen of them, and they dashed toward the stage at a full gallop, bending low over their horses. From several yards away one of the Indians shot an arrow and Marcus watched it approach, almost hypnotized by the majestic arc of its flight. At the last instant he realized the graceful-looking missile was dangerous, and he pulled aside just as the arrow thunked into the roof of the coach.

"Hold your fire!" Marcus shouted. "Hold your fire until they are right on us!"

"Whatever you say, Lieutenant. You're the Indian fighter," the guard replied.

Marcus couldn't tell him that this was his first Indian fight ever. But he knew that firing too soon would just be a waste of ammunition. If he made them wait until the war party was much closer, there would be a better chance of hitting the target when they did fire. He watched until the Indians came to within thirty yards.

"Now!" Marcus shouted. He had drawn a bead on the nearest Indian, and when he squeezed the trigger, he saw the Indian pitch from his saddle. One of the other Indians dashed right up to the side of the coach, shouting. Marcus heard the blast of the shotgun from below and he saw the Indian's face turn to pulp. A third Indian went down from the guard's rifle, and Marcus brought down a fourth.

The Indians had been totally surprised by the sudden and accurate burst of fire. Four of them went down on their initial charge and it was here, in his first skirmish, that Marcus learned a characteristic of the Indians that was both their strength and their weakness.

Though the Indians had been surprised by the spirited defense, they had no "leader," as such, to order them to withdraw and regroup. As a result, those who remained fought as ferociously as cornered wildcats. But their fighting, however vicious, was without a strategy. There were eight Indians left, but they fought as individuals, not as a unit.

The six men on the stage, on the other hand, had been formed into one cohesive fighting force by the young lieutenant. Marcus commanded the farmer and the drummer to cover the left side of the coach, the lawyer and the guard to cover the right side, while he covered the rear and the front. Every time one of the

Indians would break off for an individual charge, he would be cut down by a murderous barrage of fire from the coordinated defense of the coach.

After a running battle of no more than ten minutes, there were only three Indians left. And the Indians, though courageous, seldom pressed a battle in which the odds were against them. The three who remained, turned and galloped away with bullets whistling by just inches from their heads.

During the entire skirmish, the driver had kept the horses at a gallop. Now, with the immediate threat relieved, he pulled them to a halt and let them stand there, blowing hard in their harness.

"Whoopi!" the guard said, slapping his knee happily. "That's the best goddamned time I've ever had in my life! We was killin' them red sons of bitches like they was flies!" "You done it, Lieutenant," the driver said. "We'll be into Cheyenne Wells in another hour. Don't think they's any way the Indians can get themselves together for another attack in that time."

The Kansas Pacific Railroad track, still under construction, had reached as far as Cheyenne Wells. Because of that, Cheyenne Wells had become a "hell on wheels" end-of-track town. The population had grown much faster than the town, so that while there were a few permanent buildings, there were many more which were constructed of wood and canvas, and a fair number of plain tents. Half the business establishments in the town were saloons, thrown up to take advantage of the good pay the railroad workers were receiving.

The stagecoach pulled to a stop in front of the Railroad Hotel. Because it was so late, it drew several people to see what happened. As the driver and guard told their story, more people came, until soon, a substantial crowd was gathered around.

"Why don't the Army do somethin' about them maraudin' varmints?" someone asked. "We got a right to protection."

"Well, here's one member of the Army who did do somethin'," the guard said, pointing out Marcus. "The young lieutenant there took charge. I don't know as we woulda got through without him."

At the guard's words, the crowd which was gathered around the coach cheered and applauded. Marcus was embarrassed by the accolades, and all he wanted to do was cross the street to the railroad station and wait for the train. The lateness of the coach had not interfered with his train schedule, for the train wasn't due until midnight.

"Are you leavin' us, Lieutenant?" one of the men asked.

"Not permanently," Marcus replied. "I'm going back to New York to take charge of a platoon of new recruits. I'll be back in a couple of weeks."

"Well, it's about time the Army woke up and started sendin' us reinforcements. I'd say that calls for a drink. Come on in, Lieutenant . . . drinks are on the house."

"Thank you," Marcus said. "But I've had nothing to eat since early this morning. I believe I'd rather find a restaurant and have a meal."

"Hell, you don't have to look for no other restaurant. We serve the best steak this side of Kansas City right here in the hotel kitchen. If you won't drink with us, at least let us feed you."

Cavanaugh smiled. "All right," he said. "That's an offer I'll accept."

Marcus was swept into the Railroad Hotel with the others who had arrived on the stage. All six men were treated to a steak dinner while they were plied with questions about the Indian attack. Though Marcus was quiet about it, his role was increased by the others with each telling until he was beginning to get uncomfortable. He got anxious for the train to arrive so he could leave.

Finally he heard the welcoming sound of a train whistle. Everyone there went to the depot with him to see him onto the train and give him a hero's send-off.

"Mr. Conductor, you see to it that this young fella has everything he needs," the mayor of Cheyenne Wells said. "He's what you might call a genuine hero." The conductor was then filled in on the heroics of Second Lieutenant Marcus Cavanaugh.

"You don't worry about a thing," the conductor said. "Why, if it weren't for the brave young soldiers like the lieutenant here, the Kansas Pacific couldn't be built. Lieutenant, I want you to enjoy every moment you're on my train."

"I just need a seat in a darkened car somewhere," Marcus said. "I'm going to try and sleep until morning."

"Seat? Nothing doing. I'm going to see to it that you have a bed."

Marcus held up his travel voucher. "But my orders don't call for that," he said.

"Your orders are no good on this train, Lieutenant. I'll take care of you," the conductor promised.

Half an hour later, true to the conductor's promise, Marcus was stretched out in a bed on the sleeper car of the Midnight Flyer. In ten days he would be in New York.

2

THE ACCOLADES MARCUS HAD RECEIVED AT CHEYENNE Wells were soon dropped. When he changed trains in Kansas City he was just another passenger. The farther east he traveled the less he was welcomed. By the time he reached New York he was, because of his uniform, being regarded as a second-class citizen.

During the Civil War the military had been popular. The war used so many men that there were no families anywhere in America who didn't have some close member in uniform. That gave everyone an opinion on the military. Soldiers were "our heroes," our "brave boys in blue" or "gray." It was "When Johnny Comes Marching Home Again," and "Hurrah Boys, Hurrah!"

However, when the war ended the immediate danger to hearth and home, the military lost its support. As the nation came together again and licked its wounds, Americans— northerners and southerners —tried to forget the years of bloodshed and destruction. They didn't want to be reminded of the agony they had just gone through, and all things military were shunned. Anyone who donned a uniform was considered a ne'er-do-well ... officers and soldiers alike.

Marcus was aware of this attitude, for he had come to New York for two weeks after graduating from West Point in June of 1868. He didn't let it bother him . . . and in some ways, because he was basically a modest and private man, he preferred this treatment over the slavish hero worship he had received in Cheyenne Wells.

On the morning of the day after Marcus arrived in New York City, he stepped out of a horsecar and looked across Park Row toward the New York Times Building. Staring through the spider-web maze of telegraph wires which crossed and re-crossed the street, he could see a large sign on the building which read: American Newspaper Advertising Agency. Dozens and dozens of horsecars, carriages, wagons, and omnibuses moved up and down the street so that he had to be very careful in picking his way across. The sidewalks, like the streets, were crowded with men and women hurrying here and there, bound on some mysterious mission of commerce.

As Cavanaugh crossed the street, he heard a familiar-sounding voice. It had an Irish lilt, and belonged to a huge Irishman, six feet five or better. He seemed to be having an argument with a New York policeman.

"Come on now, you dumb mick. Don't tell me you come to the new country without a penny to your name," the policeman was saying. "You've got to have some money on you, I know you, mick."

"Sure, an' you're mistaken now, for the name isn't Mick. 'Tis Sean," the Irishman answered. "Sean O'Leary. And if I'd be havin' a cent, 'twould only be enough to keep body an' soul together until I can get a job."

"A job, is it?" the policeman asked. "Tell me, have you paid your immigration tax? You'll not be able to get a job until the immigration tax is paid."

"Glory, an' I've heard no such thing," O'Leary said. "'Twas no mention made of immigration tax when I got off the boat." "That's not my problem, is it now?" the policeman said. "How much do you have?" "Ten dollars."

"Then you're in luck. Ten dollars is how much the tax is."

Marcus could stand by no longer. "Excuse me, Officer, but I know of no such tax."

The policeman looked up angrily. "And who would you be?"

"Second Lieutenant Cavanaugh, and I'm an officer in the United States Army," Marcus said. "I have only recently graduated from the military academy and studied the immigration laws. There is no such thing as an immigration tax."

"Well, maybe you need to go back to class and be taught a new lesson," the policeman said, reaching for the nightstick on his belt.

"Hold on here," O'Leary suddenly interrupted. He

looked at Marcus. "Tell me, is it the truth ye be tellin'? This policeman has no right to ask a tax of me?"

"Butt out of this, Irishman. I'll settle your hash later," the policeman said menacingly.

"No, sir," O'Leary said. "I wouldn't be for just standin' by an' watchin' you go to work on this fine soldier on my account."

"All right, you dumb mick, then I'll start on you!" the policeman said, and he raised his club over his head, then started down toward O'Leary's head.

O'Leary reached up and clamped his hand around the policeman's wrist. The policeman, who was himself no small man, tried unsuccessfully to break the grip. O'Leary's hand squeezed down on the wrist like a steel vise. Finally, with a gasp of pain, the policeman opened his hand and dropped the club. By now, there were several others who had gathered around to watch, and there was a light applause when the club fell.

"You're in trouble now!" the policeman warned. "I'll get help and I'll run both of you in to jail."

"No, you won't," a well-dressed man in the crowd said. "We'll tell what happened." The others backed him up, and the policeman, glaring first at the crowd, and then at O'Leary and Marcus, reached down meekly to recover his club. He hooked it onto his belt, then left amid the jeers and catcalls of those who had witnessed his humiliation.

"I thank you for comin' to my assistance," O'Leary said to Marcus.

Marcus smiled and rubbed the top of his head. "I'd

say I owe you the thanks," he said. "I wouldn't have liked to be worked over with that club of his."

"Could I be botherin' you for a wee bit more?" O'Leary asked.

"If I can help."

O'Leary smiled. "Would ye be knowin' where a man with a strong back an' no fear of hard work could be findin' lawful employment?"

"No, I'm sorry, I just arrived today for . . ." Marcus rubbed his chin and looked at the big man in front of him. He was too large for the Cavalry, but the regular infantry could use him, he thought. "Are you interested in joining the Army?"

O'Leary smiled broadly. "Would your fine country be havin' the likes of me in its army?" "Come with me," Marcus invited.

The recruiting officer was a man named Captain Horner. Horner was in his late forties, overweight to the point of obesity, with a bald head and a large, brown, mutton-chop beard. The war over and peacetime promotions scarce, he was condemned to spend the rest of his career at the rank of captain at this same duty station. He was bitter about his dead-end assignment, and his bitterness had left a permanent scowl on his face.

"I'm to give you thirty men," Captain Horner said, looking at the orders Marcus handed him. He dropped them on his desk and leaned back in his chair and stroked his chin as he studied Marcus. "And just where am I supposed to come up with these thirty men, Lieutenant?"

"Sir? I don't know," Marcus replied. "I thought I was just to come here . . ."

"You thought you would just come here and get the men, with no thought of where they come from, right?" Horner asked. He leaned forward with a sigh. "It's not your fault, Cavanaugh. You are no different from the War Department. They look at the city of New York as one great, unending source of men. Well, I'll see what I can do about it. I have twenty-two men signed up now. Tomorrow is Friday, I always get a few men on Friday. Maybe I can give you what you need. Who is the big fellow who came in with you?"

Marcus looked over toward O'Leary, who was busy studying pictures on the wall of the different types of uniforms worn by the Army.

"His name is Sean O'Leary, an Irish immigrant," Marcus said. "He wants to join the Army."

"Well, that will bring it up to twenty-three. I'll only need seven more."

"But, Captain, he's too big for the Cavalry," Marcus said.

"Lieutenant, these orders call for me to furnish you with thirty men," Horner said. "They don't say anything about how big or small the men must be. Only that they be able-bodied, and there's no way you can tell me that Mr. O'Leary isn't able-bodied."

"No, sir," Marcus said. "He's able-bodied, all right."

"Then I'll swear him in. You come back here

tomorrow at eleven and I'll have your recruit platoon ready for you."

"Yes, sir," Marcus said. He saluted Captain Horner, then withdrew from his desk. Before he left the building, though, he went over to talk to Sean O'Leary.

"Would ye look at the fine-appearin' soldier suits in the pictures here?" O'Leary said. " 'Twould take a cold-hearted man not to have pride in wearin' one of these getups."

"I'm glad you feel that way, O'Leary," Marcus said. "For by this time tomorrow, you'll be Private O'Leary in my platoon. Go over there and see the captain, and he'll swear you into the Army."

O'Leary smiled broadly. "Thank you, Captain," he said, saluting.

Marcus smiled, returning his salute casually. "You're welcome—and it's 'Lieutenant,'" he said.

"Yes, Lieutenant. Whatever you say, Lieutenant, sir."

There were twenty-nine recruits sworn in when Marcus returned to the recruitment center the next day. Captain Horner had the papers on the men in a large, brown envelope, and he slid the envelope across his desk toward Marcus.

"Here they are, Lieutenant ... or at least, here is what I could come up with. Twenty- nine men, duly sworn and issued uniforms. But that's the only thing that makes them soldiers. None of them have the least bit of training . . . I'm afraid that'll be up to you when you get them to Fort Reynolds."

"Yes, sir," Marcus answered. "We'll take care of that."

"Excuse me, gentlemen," someone said. Marcus and Horner looked toward the man who had just entered. An exceptionally well dressed young man, approximately the same age as Marcus, stood just inside the door. He was about five feet eight, 140 pounds; the ideal weight and conformation for a Cavalry soldier.

"Can I help you, sir?" Captain Horner asked. Marcus thought it odd that while Horner had not called any of the other recruits "sir" before they enlisted, he did this man. But then, the appearance and demeanor of this man was considerably different from that of the others. It wasn't difficult to ascertain at once that this man was a gentleman.

"I was told that this was the office for recruitment," the new man said. "My name is Shield, William R. Shield, and I have come to offer my services." Shield held up his hand for emphasis, and when he did, he staggered a little. That was when Marcus noticed that, though well in control of himself, the young man was drunk.

"Have you been drinking?" Marcus asked.

Shield smiled. "I am not normally a man who imbibes beyond his capacity, sir. However, I must confess that, as of this moment, I am one of Bacchus's sons, yes, sir," he answered.

"Mr. Shield, are you an educated man?" Captain Horner asked.

"That, sir, depends upon your definition of the term *education*," Shield replied. "Whereas I am a graduate of Yale, class of '68, I am uneducated in the great school of life." He was silent for a moment, then added, "And, as I learned this very morning, I am particularly naive to the wiles of women. That is why, sir, I am prepared to join the United States Army." "Yes, but you would be wanting to apply for a commission. I'm afraid we can't handle that in this office. You'll have to—"

"I beg your pardon, sir, but I've come to enlist, not apply for a commission," Shield interrupted.

"Mr. Shield, might I suggest that you go home and reconsider this?" Marcus said. "If, after the drink has worn off, you still wish to—"

"Mr. Cavanaugh," Captain Horner said, coming down hard on the word *mister*. "I remind you that I am the recruiting officer here, sir, not you. If Mr. Shield wishes to be sworn in as a private I will be happy to accommodate him. And you should be, as well, for you will then have the thirty men you came for."

"But, Captain," Marcus started, only to be interrupted by Horner.

"That is all, Lieutenant. I suggest that you go outside and secure an empty omnibus. You will need it to transport your men to the railroad depot. In about five minutes they shall all be your responsibility."

"Yes, sir," Marcus said.

With a travel voucher for thirty men, thirty-one counting himself, Marcus was able to secure an entire railroad car. He sat in the rearmost seat of the car and looked over the group of recruits as the train pulled out of Grand Central Station. A large number of them were Irish, and as O'Leary had already told them the story of the lieutenant coming to his aid against the crooked policeman, the Irish of the group were disposed to respect him. Their first day and night of the trip were uneventful.

Cavanaugh knew he would need to appoint one of the men as his second-in-command for the duration of the journey, and so he spent the following morning looking over the papers to see who might help him.

"Excuse me, sir. Might I have a word with you?"

Marcus looked up to see Private Shield standing at attention in the aisle of the car. With a night's sleep sitting up in one of the hard-wooden seats, the effect of the alcohol had worn off.

"At ease, Shield," Marcus said. He sighed. "I suppose now that you have sobered up, you have come to regret your haste of yesterday, and you want me to do something about it? I'm not sure anything can be done to get you out of the Army, but I'll see what I can find out for you when we reach Fort Reynolds."

"No, sir, that's not what I want to talk about," Shield said.

"Yes, Private?"

"I wasn't so drunk that I don't remember you trying to help me yesterday," Shield said. "And for that, I thank you. But I want to tell you that even now, in my sobered state, this is what I want."

"Are you sure, Shield? Being a horse soldier on the western frontier isn't like being a student at Yale University. It isn't even like being a cadet at West Point. It's nothing like the life you are leaving behind."

"That is my earnest desire, sir," Shield said. "You see, I want nothing of the life I've left behind, nor anything to remind me of it." "And so you are using the Army to escape?" "Is that so new, sir?" Shield asked. "I've read that the Army is a haven for society's outcasts and runaways. Thieves, extortioners, bigamists, even murderers I'm told, have fled their past by donning army blue."

"Too true, I regret to say."

"And some, I've read, have made very good soldiers."

"Yes," Marcus said. Though he had not been in the Army long enough to speak of that from personal experience, he had heard of such things. "Which are you, Shield?"

"I am neither thief, bigamist, nor murderer," Shield said. "But I do have compelling reasons for wishing to start a new life. I was faced with the dilemma of forfeiting either my honor or my soul."

Marcus held up his hand. "You don't have to tell me anything if you don't want to," he said. "In the Army, we take a man at face value."

"Thank you," Shield replied. "But I do want to tell you this ... I feel you are a man I can trust."

"All right," Marcus said.

"I was engaged to be married," Shield said. He smiled sadly. "In fact, we were to have been married ... this very afternoon. But yesterday morning I found the woman I was to marry—and her lover—in a most compromising position. I'm sure that pride and manly honor dictated that I call out her lover and kill him. But I couldn't do that. I couldn't do that, you see, because her lover is my own brother." Marcus looked at the young man and saw the pain in his eyes. The young lieutenant had never known a woman's love and had, in fact, taken a private oath while still at West Point to let the Army be his only mistress. Marcus's mother had died when he was a small boy. His father, a judge from Michigan, had used his influence to secure an appointment to the academy, but had died during his son's first year. Marcus was alone now, but he had no sense of being lonely. He had a family . . . the largest family a man could possibly want. His family was the United States Army. Perhaps it could do the same thing for William R. Shield.

"Shield, I need an acting corporal for the duration of this trip," Marcus said. "Would you assume that responsibility?"

Shield smiled, then came to attention. "I would be most honored," he said.

"Lieutenant Cavanaugh?"

Marcus opened his eyes. It had been a long and tiring trip, and for ten days he had tried to find some way to make the seat more comfortable. That he was asleep was more a testimony to his exhaustion than to any degree of success. "Yes?"

"We're coming into Cheyenne Wells," Shield said. I believe you said that was where we would detrain."

Marcus sat up and rubbed his eyes, then looked out through the window at the now-familiar plains of eastern Colorado.

"Yes," he said. "This is where we get off. Are the men ready?"

"Yes, sir." Shield smiled. "If you ask me, they're more than anxious to get off. What happens next?"

Marcus shaped his hat, then put it on his head. He looked up at Shield and smiled. "I'm not sure," he said. "But don't tell the men that. I wouldn't want them to ever think their lieutenant isn't sure about everything."

Shield laughed, as much in appreciation of being let in on the secret as the joke.

"I sent a telegram from Junction City," Marcus went on. "My hope is that they have made some arrangement for transporting us from Cheyenne Wells to the fort."

As they detrained, Marcus saw three Army wagons, with drivers and escorts, waiting at the depot platform. A young, black-haired, blue-eyed second lieutenant, his face dusted with freckles, came up to Marcus and saluted. As Marcus was also only a second lieutenant, the action took him by surprise. The young officer was a complete stranger to him.

"I am Second Lieutenant John Culpepper, sir, here with the transport and escort for your platoon," the young man said.

"At ease, Lieutenant," Marcus said, returning his salute. "We're the same rank."

"No, sir. You rank me by six weeks, sir," Culpepper said. "Whereas you graduated from West Point in June, I received a direct appointment from the secretary of war in August. After a short wait for my orders, I was posted to Fort Reynolds in your absence." Marcus smiled broadly and shook the young man's hand. "Well, I must say I'm glad to see you," he said. "Not only because you've brought our transportation, but also, because I will no longer be the junior officer on post." "Yes, sir, I thought that would make you happy."

"Come on, Culpepper. Let's save the formal address for the fort."

"Captain Forsyth said you were a decent fellow," Culpepper said. "But you never can tell how it's going to be when you meet someone with the kind of reputation you have." "Reputation?" Marcus asked, puzzled by the remark. "What do you mean, 'reputation'?"

"Well, you know, hero and all that."

"I don't have the slightest idea of what you are talking about."

"You don't? Why, it's all over Fort Reynolds . . . no, it's all over Colorado, how you organized the men on the stagecoach to fight off Two Eagles and thirty warriors."

Marcus shook his head. "There were never more than ten or twelve," he said. "And, though I wouldn't know Two Eagles if I saw him, I would be willing to bet he wasn't one of them."

"That's not what it says in the newspapers." "The newspapers!"

"You bet. You've been written about in every newspaper out here. You're a hero, Cavanaugh. A real hero."

"Don't believe everything you read in the newspapers," Marcus said. "Now, what are your orders?"

"My orders are to bring the transport and escort detail to Cheyenne Wells and present myself to you for further instructions."

"Very well," Marcus said. "Let's get the men loaded and out of here before they discover that every other building in this entire town is a saloon."

The fort band was turned out to welcome Cavanaugh and the new recruits. Marcus, who was riding one of the horses, hurried back to the wagons to make certain each man was sitting at attention as they entered the post. Captain Forsyth was standing under the flagpole, and Marcus led the group over to him, halted them, then reported.

"Lieutenant Cavanaugh returning with recruits as ordered, sir," he barked, snapping a salute. Forsyth, in addition to being the third-ranking man on the post, was also Cavanaugh's company commander.

"Well done, Lieutenant, well done," Forsyth said. "You can turn the men over to the sergeants here. I'm sure they'll take good care of them. Then, if you would, the colonel asks that we join him for a drink at the sutler's."

"Yes, sir," Marcus said. A couple of sergeants arrived then and took charge of the men to show them to the barracks and the stables. Their official training would start tomorrow, with Marcus in charge.

Marcus followed Captain Forsyth over to the sutler's store. The sutler's store, in addition to acting as a general store, was also, in rooms segregated for officers and enlisted, a place for the men to go for relaxation.

The sutler extended credit, protected by the fact that it would be deducted from the pay of the enlisted men. Officers, on the other hand, were allowed to run up personal tabs as a privilege of rank independent of their monthly pay.

"Hail, the conquering hero returns," Pettibone said. There was just a trace of sarcasm in his voice, enough to make Marcus somewhat uneasy.

"I would hardly consider myself a hero, Colonel Pettibone, let alone a conquering hero."

"Oh? Well, that isn't the way I read it," Pettibone said. "You've been in every paper between here and the Mississippi River. Some of the papers, I hear, are calling on the governor of Colorado to appoint you a colonel in the Colorado Militia. I wouldn't be surprised if the good citizens didn't petition to have you take command of all military forces within the Colorado borders."

"Colonel, I don't understand all of this," Marcus said. "We were attacked by a small war party. ..."

"Small?" Pettibone asked. "You mean it wasn't the entire Cheyenne nation?"

"No, sir. It was no more than ten or twelve." "To your six. Still a heroic action."

"We were well armed, sir. The Cheyenne were not."

"Yes, well, nevertheless, you did perform admirably, and for that, you have my congratulations." Pettibone held up his glass. "I drink a toast to you, Lieutenant, and to your successful trip. You did get thirty new men?"

"Yes, sir."

"Good. Tomorrow you will begin their training. Oh, and I will expect that training to include Lieutenant Culpepper as well. Unlike you, Mr. Culpepper has not had the privilege of West Point. His commission came by political appointment. With the disgrace his father brought upon himself, I can hardly see how young Culpepper was able to find anyone to sponsor his cause."

"What do you mean, sir?"

"Surely you have heard of his father, Lieutenant? General Henry Lee Culpepper? And his grandfather, General Ambrose Culpepper?"

"Yes, sir," Marcus said. "I studied the tactics of the elder at the academy. I did not realize Lieutenant Culpepper was related."

"He didn't tell you?"

"No, sir."

"Well, I'm not surprised. Henry Lee Culpepper gave up his commission to become a general for Robert E. Lee. I do not understand why West Point would bother to teach the tactics of the father of a traitor."

"Surely you remember tactics classes, Colonel. We study all brilliant military leaders, without regard to politics, from Caesar and Atilla the Hun to Napoleon and General Lafayette."

"Yes, well, now is your chance to turn the tables," Pettibone said. "You studied Culpepper, now a Culpepper will study you." Pettibone stood quickly, and Marcus and Forsyth stood with him. "Please, gentlemen, please," he said. "Stay and enjoy your drink. I have work to do."

Both officers stood until Pettibone was gone, then, at Forsyth's invitation, Marcus sat down again. Forsyth chuckled.

"What is it, sir?"

"My boy, you made a primary mistake," Forsyth said. "You allowed yourself to become better known than your commander."

"Believe me, Captain, it wasn't my doing," Marcus said.

"Oh, I believe you. But the truth is, your action did bring credit upon the Army and Pettibone knows it. And as much as he is jealous that it is Marcus Cavanaugh and not Andrew Pettibone who is getting all the credit, he is also aware that the publicity is good for the Army. And for all his faults, he is Army enough to accept that. For the present, at least."

"I'd give anything if it hadn't happened," Marcus said.

"I'm glad it did happen," Forsyth said, and this time there was a more serious expression on his face. He took a swallow of his beer. "Marcus, we're sitting on a powder keg out here. Two Eagles is going to come busting out of his reservation sometime soon, and when he does he's going to have every buck between the Mississippi River and the Rocky Mountains with him. It's good to know that I have someone I can count on."

"Captain, that was the first time in my life I had ever been under fire," Marcus said. "If you are looking to me for experience, I'm afraid I've none to offer."

"Lieutenant, the fact that it was your first time and you handled it as well as you did speaks very well for you. Experience be damned. It doesn't mean a thing unless there is courage and common sense to go with it. No, sir, Pettibone might be peeved at your little heroic episode, but not I. I've no doubt but that you will do very well when it comes down to it. And the young lad, Culpepper, as well. Of course, I've nothing to base that on except his breeding, but I've always been a believer that bloodlines will tell."

"Yes, sir," Marcus said.

Forsyth finished his beer, then wiped the back of his hand across his mouth. "Now, if we could only count on Major Conklin," he said.

Marcus looked over toward the executive officer who, sitting at the last table in the room, was already into his cups. It had been whispered, even at the academy, that one of the most severe problems facing the Army today was the alcoholism of its officers. Conklin, overage in grade and probably destined to remain there forever, was one such officer. He seldom drew a sober breath as he waited patiently for his years of service to go by so he could be pensioned out.

"He was a good man once," Forsyth said. He sighed. "But that was a long time ago."

"I wish I had known him then," Marcus said. This was awkward for him. Conklin was still his superior officer, even if he was a drunk, and he felt uncomfortable talking about him in such a way.

"Oh, did I tell you? Missouri Joe will be coming to the fort next month," Forsyth said.

Marcus smiled. "So, at long last I get to meet the illustrious Mr. Missouri Joe, the best scout in the Army."

"Well, according to Missouri Joe he's the best," Forsyth said, then he laughed. "The thing is, he's probably right."

3

"Boy, what you a standin' there for? Move outta my way, else I'll set my squaw onto you." "I'm sorry, sir, this is U.S. goverment oats." "That's all right, boy, I'm a U.S. government scout."

Marcus had been working with the new recruits for one month now and was at the rear of the stable watching them going through equipment drill when he heard the conversation between the guard and someone at the front of the barn. When he looked around to see what was going on, he saw one of the new men holding a rifle at port arms, trying to protect the platoon's store of oats from two civilians. One was a tall, scarecrow- thin man with long white hair and a full, white beard, and the other was the biggest and the ugliest Indian woman Marcus had ever seen. The woman was scowling at the young soldier, who was staring nervously back at her. When the man, who was dressed in buckskin, saw Marcus, he spit a wad of tobacco out before he talked.

"Lieutenant, best you tell this here boy who I am." He squinted at Marcus. "That is, *if* you know who I am. Don't believe you was around when I left last spring."

"No, sir, I had not yet arrived. It's all right, Barnes," Marcus said to the young soldier. "Unless I miss my guess, this is Missouri Joe." "Well, now, you'd be pretty smart for a shavetail," the scout said.

"I'll accept that as a compliment."

"Yes, well, you should. That there is how I meant it. Now, do you mind if I take the pack offen the mule an' turn it into the stable?" "No, go ahead," Marcus invited.

"I'll get it for you," Barnes offered, and the young recruit walked over to the mule, then began straining with the pack.

Missouri Joe chuckled. "Somethin' wrong, boy?" he asked.

"No, sir. It's just a little too heavy for one man, is all."

"Moon Cow Woman," Missouri Joe said. She grunted what might have been an acknowledgment, then walked over and lifted the cargo pack from the back of the mule, handling it as easily as if she were removing a buffalo robe. Barnes looked on with his eyes wide in wonder.

"What would be your name, boy?" Missouri Joe asked, turning his attention back to Marcus.

"I am Lieutenant Cavanaugh."

The Indian woman looked around, her face

suddenly becoming animated. She spoke in a quick, harsh language, and somewhere in her short speech, Marcus clearly heard the word "Cavanaugh."

"Did she say my name?" Marcus asked. "That's right, boy, she surely did. She said you sure was a pretty man an' she hoped Two Eagles wouldn't be able to keep his vow to kill you."

Marcus blinked in surprise. "Two Eagles has made a vow to kill me. . . personally?" "That's right, boy. That's quite a honor, you know. You prob'ly don't know this, but a man who is a great enemy to the Indian is just as much a hero to them as someone who is a great friend. Yes, sir, the Cheyenne say your name in all their tepees just about ever' night. Whoever kills you will have big medicine." "I'd just as soon not be a hero to them," Marcus said.

Missouri Joe chuckled. "It's too late for that, boy. It's too late."

Several of the recruits who had been learning to saddle their horses now drifted toward the front of the barn. They hung back in the shadows, looking at Missouri Joe and at the Indian woman who was with him. She was at least six feet tall and weighed well over two hundred pounds. Missouri Joe saw them, then he laughed and walked over and put his arm around Moon Cow Woman. Her large, flat face broke into a wide smile, and she put her arms around him and picked him up, holding him about six inches off the ground as she embraced him. Some of the soldiers laughed and elbowed each other.

"Boys," Missouri Joe said to them. "I know what you be a' thinkin'. You be a' thinkin' this here is the ugliest one woman any of you have ever seed. Right?"

The men looked at each other nervously, but no one answered.

"Hell, don't be shy. I admit it. She's one ugly woman."

Now a few of the men agreed, and they shook their heads.

"Well, boys, let me tell you somethin'. Iffen I want beauty, I'll look at the sunset. Ain't nothin' on God's green earth any prettier than a sunset out in the wild. But this here woman sleeps warm and breeds good. And she can do the work of any three of you. So if you don't mind, I'll leave all the pretty women to the drawin' room dandies, and I'll take me a woman like Moon Cow Woman anytime."

Colonel Pettibone's wife, Martha, and Amy Lapes, wife of the post surgeon, co-hosted a dinner that night at the commandant's quarters. Though they were the hostesses, the other officers' wives who were on the post, Drusilla Conklin, Janet Forsyth, and a few others, had pitched in by supplying silver, crystal, and china. And as the goods available for purchase at the sutler's store were strictly rationed, they shared that as well, bringing together their smoked oysters, canned peaches, and other delicacies to create quite a good meal.

"I asked Missouri Joe if he would dine with us

tonight," Captain Forsyth said over the dinner table. "But he said he would rather eat his squaw's cooking."

"Oh, heavens, that terrible man?" Martha said. "And has anyone taken a good look at that creature he calls his wife?" The other women laughed.

"Martha's right. It's just as well he didn't accept," Pettibone said. "The man has no manners, no culture, and who knows how long it has been since he has taken a bath?" "Wouldn't you like to be closed up with him in a stuffy room?" Mrs. Lapes quipped, and again, the ladies laughed.

"Nevertheless, sir, you must admit that he is an invaluable source of information," Forsyth said. "Living with the Indians as he does, he has almost become one of them."

"Yes, and I don't mind saying that that is one of the things that bothers me," Pettibone said. "I have a hard time believing that a man who lives like he does can know who his friends are. Who is to say that any information he gives us is accurate?"

"Colonel, if you'll forgive me for saying so," Forsyth said, "Missouri Joe knows where his duty lies."

"Nevertheless, I intend to take all of his information with a grain of salt," Pettibone said.

"Surely we can find something more pleasant to talk about at the dinner table than that dirty old man," Martha said. She turned to Marcus and smiled brightly. "Lieutenant Cavanaugh, were you able to enjoy any plays while you were in New York?"

"No, ma'am," Marcus answered. "I was only there for one day, I'm afraid."

"Heavens! How can anyone go to New York without taking advantage of all the wonderful things there are to do in the city?"

"Now, Martha," Pettibone said, "Lieutenant Cavanaugh isn't like you. He has an appreciation for duty. He was in New York on orders, and they didn't include seeing the latest theatrical."

"Nevertheless, it would have been good had he gone," Martha said. "Then he could have shared the play with us."

"I do miss the theater so," Drusilla said. She was a small, birdlike woman who may have been very pretty at one time. The rigors of continuous service in the Far West, plus the burden of living with a husband who, because of his alcoholic indulgence, was only "half-there" most of the time, had told on her so that, though only forty, she looked much closer to sixty.

"Perhaps I can arrange to have one of those traveling theatrical groups visit Fort Reynolds sometime," Pettibone suggested.

"Oh, Andrew, that would be wonderful," Martha said.

"In the meantime, we have important business to attend to out here," Pettibone said. He looked across the table at Marcus, then smiled. "Well, Lieutenant, tomorrow is the big day for you and your platoon, isn't it? You're taking them out on a three-day scout."

"Yes, sir," Marcus said.

"I want you to ride up to the North Fork of Smokey Hill Creek. Take a look around up there, then come on back."

"Beg your pardon, sir, but Missouri Joe said Two Eagles had a hunting camp up that way," Forsyth said.

"Yes, I know."

"Then, don't you think it is unwise to send Marcus and his men up there? Especially as Marcus is now big medicine to whatever Indian might kill him."

"That's what happens when you become a hero," Pettibone said. Then he laughed, as if dismissing it. "But really, thirty men, well-armed, and two officers? Captain, if it has come down to the point that we are unable to operate in the countryside with an entire platoon, then something is drastically wrong." "Maybe so, sir. But these men are all raw recruits."

"Ah, but Marcus has already had his baptism of fire," Pettibone said.

"Sir, request permission to accompany the platoon," Captain Forsyth said.

"Permission denied, Captain. I have need of you on the post. Anyway, if we can't count on the leadership ability of our lieutenants now, when can we count on them? Don't worry, I'm absolutely certain that there is nothing up there at all. And if there is, why, by Missouri Joe's own words, it is nothing more than a minor hunting camp . . . probably abandoned by now."

"Captain Forsyth, I want to go," Marcus said.

"Me, too," Culpepper added.

"You see there, Captain?" Pettibone said, smiling

and preening his mustache. "Your young officers are full of self-confidence." Forsyth let out a long sigh, realizing that he was licked. He ran his hand through his hair. "Very well, then at least let me send a few seasoned men along with them," he said. "A corporal for each squad and Sergeant Flynn. He's been working with the lieutenants and the recruits."

"Very well, Captain, I see no problem with that. And now, gentlemen," he went on, "if you would, please, charge your glasses. I propose a toast to the successful mission of our two young lieutenants. Major Conklin? You'll drink with us, sir?"

Drusilla, embarrassed by the fact that her husband had been sitting beside her in an alcoholic haze for the entire meal, paying no attention whatever to what was going on, punched him in the side with her elbow. At her nudge, Conklin looked up from a plate that was virtually untouched. For a moment his eyes swam in their sockets as he tried to focus, then, when he saw everyone raising their glasses, he smiled, refilled his own, and raised it with the others.

"Hear, hear," he gurgled. Drusilla looked down in shame while the other wives avoided looking at her.

Back in his own quarters after dinner, Marcus went over the map for the third time. He had discussed every point with Captain Forsyth: the location of all the fords, the gullies and ravines that could be crossed with no difficulty, and those that couldn't. He had also marked out the exact location of the hunting camp, according to Missouri Joe.

He laid the map aside and began seeing to his gear, when there was a knock on his door. When he opened it, he saw the smiling, eager face of John Culpepper.

"Culpepper come in. Have you got your gear together?"

"Yes, I'm all ready to go," John said. "Cavanaugh, I don't mind telling you, I'm very excited about this. It will be great to get out of the post for a while, and away from the constant drills."

"You aren't worried about the hunting camp Missouri Joe told us about?"

"Not at all," John said. "I figure if it's there, we'll handle it." He reached inside his jacket pocket. "I have something for you."

"For me? What?"

"You remember I told you I had a sister? She's eighteen and she doesn't look at all like me. She's pretty."

Marcus chuckled. "Fortunately it usually works out that way. . . the sisters get all the looks in a family," he said.

"Well, anyway, I told her all about you, and she sent this letter for me to give to you." Self-consciously, he handed Marcus the envelope. "As you can see, it's sealed. . . I didn't read it."

"John, I don't know . . ."

"Look, I'm not trying to play Cupid or anything like that," John said. "It's just that"— he stopped and looked down at the floor for a minute, embarrassed by what he was about to say—"It's just that I know you don't have anyone to write to. . . no mother or father, no sisters or brothers. And, by your own admission, no girl, either. I don't know how you can take the loneliness without having someone. Anyhow, I thought, well, maybe if you could just sort of write to Sally every now and then, why, I'm sure she would answer your letters. And it might help sometime for you to have someone away from the post to talk to."

Marcus smiled and took the letter.

"All right, John, you win," he said. "But I certainly hope you haven't built me up too high in your sister's eyes."

"I. . . uh, I'll get back over to my own quarters now and let you read it."

"Thanks'" Marcus said. "See you at reveille." Marcus went back to his desk and sat down under the kerosene lamp. He looked at the envelope and at the neat and obviously feminine penmanship of the address. When he took out his knife to open it, he thought he caught a whiff of perfume and, for a moment, he thought back to West Point. He recalled the girls who came to the dances in their colorful, swirling dresses. Wherever they went they left a flowery scent behind them, floating over the dance floor, or hanging in the air as they strolled down flirtation walk with the cadets.

Putting that thought behind him, Marcus began to read:

"Dear Lieutenant Cavanaugh,

You must think it terribly bold of me to write to you in this fashion. In fact, it is quite bold, and if I thought I ever would actually meet you sometime, I'm quite sure I wouldn't have the nerve to do this. However, my brother has spoken so highly of you that I feel certain that you will take these letters in the light they are meant, and not think me forward for initiating a correspondence.

John seems to think that, as you have no one at home, a few letters might bring you comfort. If he is correct in his assumption I shall be glad to provide that service. If, however, you do not wish to hear from me again, just disregard this letter and, if it receives no answer, I will understand.

I am eighteen years old. I have blond hair and blue eyes. I love to dance and play the piano. I also enjoy riding horses, though mother tells me that my appreciation of horses is unladylike.

May I confess something to you? I would like to use these letters as a diary. I have never kept a diary, but I have friends who do. I've always thought a diary was rather foolish, for what is the sense of writing if no one is going to read what is written? On the other hand, there are times when certain things ought to be said, thoughts should be expressed. Therefore, if you are agreeable, I shall let you be my diary.

Good luck to you, Lieutenant Cavanaugh.

Your friend,

Sally Culpeper"

Marcus looked at the letter for a few moments, then he smiled, folded it back into the envelope, and put it in his inside jacket pocket. Why not answer her? He would tell her clearly, in his first letter, of his vow of bachelorhood for the duration of his Army career. If she wanted him to be her diary, then she, too, could be a means of expressing his own thoughts. Perhaps John was right. Perhaps having someone to exchange letters with would be good.

Getting out a paper and pen, Marcus answered Sally's letter, telling her he would very much like to exchange letters with her. "And as for being your diary, Miss Culpepper, I would deem it an honor to serve in such a capacity. You may rest assured that I will never divulge the slightest thing told me in confidence."

After the letter was finished, Marcus took an evening walk outside. Under the full moon, the Arkansas River was a stream of molten silver winding its way through the low hills of eastern Colorado.

Fort Reynolds was like a painting in soft shades of silver and black. Only the commandant's house escaped the unifying brush of evening to glisten a brilliant white in the moonlight, its cupolas, turrets, and bay windows sprouting from it like blooms on a desert cactus.

Out on the quadrangle, a twelve-pounder signal cannon and a flagpole with its banner struck for the night, gleamed softly. On the opposite side of the parade ground lay a long, low row of unpainted houses. These were the quarters for enlisted men who were married. Most of them were dark, though here and there a flickering light managed to escape. The enlisted men couldn't afford kerosene lanterns so such lights, Marcus knew, were likely to come from homemade lamps of rag and grease or tallow dip. They were dim and smoky and gave off a thick odor.

It wasn't just the light that made the air heavy here. These dark, mean little houses were called "Soapsuds Row," and that was an appropriate name for the area north of the quadrangle, for many of the enlisted men's wives were also laundresses. The laundresses received five dollars a month to do an officer's laundry and two dollars for an enlisted man. Laundresses at Fort Reynolds numbered one to every nineteen and a half soldiers, and the evidence of their day's work was the permanent smell of lye, bleach, and wood ash that scented the air.

This evening Marcus thought the scent was particularly pungent. The night air held it, as it held the long, high-pitched trills and low viola like thrums of the frogs. For countermelody, there were the crickets in the distance; the long, mournful howl of the coyotes; and from the stable, a mule braying and a horse whickering.

From the sutler's store a wedge of lantern light spilled through the open door and splashed over the boardwalk. The sutlers could afford coal oil for their lanterns and they could sell beer. Tonight the sutler's store was doing a brisk business.

Marcus walked out into the middle of the quadrangle. Above him, stars shimmered like crystals in the dark vault of sky. From a distant barracks he could hear a soldier's ballad; high, clear and sweet: "I'll Take You Home Again, Kathleen." Then he saw a soldier coming toward him, holding a trumpet.

"Good evenin', Lieutenant," the soldier said, saluting.

"Good evening," Marcus replied, returning the salute. He leaned against the signal cannon then and watched as the trumpeter raised the instrument to his lips. The trumpeter blew air through it a couple of times to clear it, then he began to play taps. Marcus listened to the mournful notes as they filled the night air, calling the soldiers to bed. They rolled out across the flat open parade ground, hitting the low hills beyond the walls of the fort, then bouncing back a second later in a haunting echo. Of all the military rituals, taps was the most stirring. From his first night at West Point, he had never heard it without feeling a chill. He remembered the often-unsung words:

Day is done.

Gone the sun

From the lake

From the hill From the sky.

Rest in peace Soldier brave God is nigh....

The next morning the entire post was turned out for Marcus's departure. The officers and men who were not going had been given temporary leave of their duties to form into a regimental parade front around the quadrangle. Marcus was on horseback, standing in his stirrups. For the moment there was absolute silence. The only sound that could be heard was the snapping and flapping of the garrison flag, flying high overhead.

Marcus surveyed the assembled platoon of thirty mounted cavalrymen, sitting tall and proud in their saddles, stretched out in a long single line facing him. Lieutenant Culpepper and Sergeant Flynn were mounted outside the line, between Marcus and the troopers.

"Lieutenant Culpepper, prepare to move out!" Marcus shouted to John, who, for this training patrol, was his second-in-command. John turned to face the men.

"Company, form column of twos!" he yelled, his voice echoing across the fort.

The men, having learned the procedure during their month of training, executed the command.

"Guidon post!" Culpepper yelled, and a soldier carrying a red-and-white pennant galloped to the head of the column.

Colonel Pettibone rode up to the flagpole and halted.

"Sir," Culpepper said, saluting and reporting to Marcus. "The company is formed."

"Thank you, Lieutenant," Marcus said, returning John's salute. Marcus turned to face Pettibone and saluted sharply.

"Colonel, I have the honor, sir, of reporting that the company is ready for your command."

"Excercise your marching order, Lieutenant," Pettibone replied, returning Marcus's salute.

Marcus turned back toward Lieutenant Culpepper. Never in his life, not even on the day he graduated from West Point, had he felt a greater swell of pride than at this moment. This was his first command, and he fixed it in his mind so he could recall it any time he wished. It was suspended in time and space for all eternity.

"Move them out, Lieutenant," Marcus said quietly.

Lieutenant Culpepper stood high in his stirrups. "Forward, ho!" he yelled.

The company started through the gates while, beneath the flagpole, the regimental band began playing "The Girl I Left Behind Me."

Pettibone retired from the field then and joined the ladies who had gathered at the sally port to watch as Marcus's men passed by.

As the company passed, Marcus drew his saber and gave the command, "Eyes right!" He held the hilt of the sword at his chin, with the blade pointing up and out at a forty-five-degree angle, then turned his head to the right to pay his respects to the officers and their ladies. Pettibone returned his salute. Marcus held it until they were passed, then he returned his saber to the scabbard as they rode through the gates.

4

THEY HAD BEEN ON THE TRAIL FOR AN HOUR THE NEXT morning, moving slowly but steadily across the east Colorado plains. The ground stretched out before them in folds of hills, one after another. As each ridge was crested another was exposed, and beyond that, another still. The dusty grass gave off a pungent, earthy smell when crushed by the hooves of the horses.

The soft light of dawn had long since given way to the white brightness of midmorning, and already the sun promised another long, hot day. It was now late September, though, and Marcus knew from talking to the old hands that the winter would be brutal. They told him of days when all the creatures, wild and domestic, would herd together in pitiful clumps, starving and freezing to death in broad fields of white.

Marcus held his hand up to bring the column to a halt.

"Sergeant Flynn, give the men and horses a short blow. Lieutenant Culpepper, come with me."

At Flynn's order, the soldiers dismounted and walked their horses to cool them down. Some of the soldiers stretched out on the ground for a moment while several others took the opportunity to relieve themselves.

Cavanaugh and Culpepper climbed up the side of a hill, where Marcus used his binoculars to scan the horizon. He saw only dusty rocks, shimmering grass, and more ranges of hills under the beating sun. He started to drop the glasses when he saw one outcropping of rock that looked different from the others. He stared at it more closely.

"John," he said, handing the glasses over. "Am I just seeing things, or is that a burned- out wagon?"

The officer took the glasses and looked in the direction Marcus had pointed. "It's a wagon, all right."

"I don't recall Missouri Joe saying anything about a burned-out wagon this route, do you?" "No," John said. "I don't." He lowered the glasses. "Why don't we ask Flynn?"

"Good idea. Sergeant Flynn!" he shouted.

Sergeant Flynn ran up the hill, puffing loudly by the time he reached the two officers. "Yes, sir, what is it?" he asked.

"Take a look, Sergeant," Marcus said as John handed him the glasses. "Unless Lieutenant Culpepper and I are mistaken, that's a burned-out wagon ahead."

Flynn held the glasses to his eyes, adjusting the

focus. "Yes, sir, I'd say that's what it is." "Have you seen it before?" Marcus said. "No, sir," Flynn said. "There wasn't nothin' like that last time I was through here, an' that couldn't have been more'n a couple of months ago. That's got to be a recent ..." Sergeant Flynn paused. He lowered the glasses slowly and pinched the bridge of his nose. "Sweet, sweet Jesus," he said again.

"What is it, Sergeant Flynn? What do you see?" Marcus asked.

Flynn handed the glasses back to Marcus. "Look behind the wagon, Lieutenant. 'Bout thirty yards or so."

Marcus looked at the wagon again, then moved the binoculars to the back. There, lying on the ground, he saw two clumps of red. "What is it, Lieutenant?" John asked. Marcus let out a slow breath of air, then handed the glasses back to John.

"Bodies, Mr. Culpepper," he said. "Two women. Look for the red. That's the color of the dresses they are wearing. At least this time the savages left the women clothed. That was more than they did at the stagecoach station." John looked again, then drew in a short gasp as he saw them.

"Would the lieutenant be for wantin' a closer look?" Sergeant Flynn asked.

"Yes, Sergeant. Let's get the men mounted," Marcus said.

Flynn hurried back down the hill.

"All right, you men, it's back in the saddles with you, now! We've a bit of somethin' that must be checked out."

"And would it be some action we'll be seein', Sergeant Flynn?"

"Don't ye be worryin' none about seein' action, trooper," Flynn replied. "I'm thinkin' you'll be seein' more'n you've a mind to before you've finished your time with the Fourth." "Forward at a trot," Marcus called after he'd mounted.

The column broke into a trot. Sabers, canteens, mess kits, and rifles jangled under the irregular rhythm of the trotting horses, and dust boiled up behind them. Marcus held the trot until they were within a hundred yards of the wagon.

"At a gallop!" Marcus called as he stood in his stirrups and drew his saber, pointing it forward. The saber wasn't drawn as a weapon, but rather as a signaling device, for a drawn saber meant that carbines should be pulled from the saddle scabbard and held at the ready.

Every nerve in Marcus's body was tingling as the group of soldiers swept down on the scene. The young lieutenant was alert to every blade of grass, every rock and stone, every hill and gully. He was not about to be ambushed by Indians.

They reached the wagon and Marcus held up his hand, calling them to a halt.

"Line of skirmishers, front and rear!" Marcus called, and two squads of horse soldiers moved into position.

Marcus swung down from his horse, as did Culpepper, but Marcus held up his hand, stopping him.

"No, Lieutenant. The regulations say that when a

patrol is on scout in a suspicious area, the commander and the second-in-command should never dismount at the same time. One of us has to be ready to assume mounted command."

"Of course. I'm sorry," Culpepper said. There was an edge of excitement in John's voice, but not fear. Marcus found it reassuring. If something happened, he was certain John would be ready.

Cavanaugh walked toward the two red clumps on the ground. As he approached, he could hear the buzzing of flies. He stopped just before he reached them and braced himself for what he was about to see.

It was a woman and a little girl, lying side by side in the grass. The only wounds visible were gunshot wounds in the head. A short distance behind the wagon, Marcus saw a man lying on his back. The man was stripped naked, and the top of his head was bashed in. He had been bald, and the Indians, as if taking out their frustration at the lack of a scalp, had opened his cranium to allow the brains to spill out onto the ground. His penis and testicles had been cut off, as had the ring finger on his left hand. There were large gashes on his thighs, his abdomen was open, and his heart had been cut out.

Marcus didn't have to be an old hand to figure out what had happened here. A wagon, traveling alone, had been attacked by the Indians. The man had been killed and the woman had killed the little girl and then herself. Her hand was till shaped as if around a pistol, though the Indians had taken the gun, so that her hand, stiffened by rigor mortis, resembled a grotesque claw.

"Sergeant Flynn, assign a burial detail," Marcus ordered as he walked back to the horses.

"Aye, sir," Flynn said. "O'Leary, Burgess, Keogh," he called. The men, whether moved by a morbid curiosity or a decent inclination to bury the victims, took their shovels without protest and began digging the graves.

Marcus looked over at O'Leary, who stood head and shoulders taller than the other men. Marcus was surprised that Pettibone had let the big man stay in the Cavalry. He thought the regimental commander would give him some type of garrison duty. But O'Leary wanted to be with the horse soldiers, and the cavalrymen wanted him with them, seeming to take some comfort in his size and strength. The stable sergeant managed to come up with an oversized horse that was stronger than average, and O'Leary had been keeping up with the others quite well during this patrol.

"Beggin' your pardon, Lieutenant," Flynn said. "But did you notice anythin' about the bodies?"

"What do you mean?"

"They wasn't swole up none by the sun." "What are you getting at, Sergeant?" Culpepper asked.

"I think I know," Marcus said. "The sergeant means this didn't happen too long ago." "That's right, sir. I'm thinkin' these poor souls was kilt no longer ago than this very mornin'. Maybe a couple of hours ago at the most."

"Lieutenant Cavanaugh, we found something," Shield called from near the wagon.

Marcus walked over to Shield, and the soldier handed him a small ledger.

"What is that?" Marcus said.

"Evidently the little girl was keeping a diary, sir," Shield said.

Marcus opened it up and read aloud from the front page: "'The Personal Account of an Exciting Trip West, by Amy Johnson, Age Twelve.'"

"It was excitin', all right," Sergeant Flynn said quietly.

"'July fifteenth, 1868, Sikeston, Missouri. My father has just informed us that we are leaving Missouri and going west to have a farm of our own. Mama is very sad but I am very excited,'" Marcus read. He look at the words on the page, neatly Filling the spaces between the lines, as if the young girl were working hard on her penmanship. He cleared his throat, unable to go on. He closed the book and looked back toward the three graves. By now the bodies, wrapped in what bit of canvas there was remaining from the wagon cover, had been lowered into the holes. The burial detail was covering them with dirt. When they were finished and nothing remained but three mounds, O'Leary stood up and crossed himself. Many of the others followed suit.

"What do we do now, Lieutenant Cavanaugh?" John asked. "Are you going back?"

"We were told to go all the way to the fork of the river, and that's what we're going to do," Marcus said.

"Sergeant Flynn, order the trumpeter to sound boots and saddles," Lieutenant Culpepper said.

"Yes, sir," Flynn said.

Fifi

The trumpeter blew the call which summoned the soldiers to their horses, and a few minutes later the column was on the march again. They maintained a steady pace for the rest of the day and finally reached their destination just before nightfall. Sergeant Flynn assigned a detail to see to the horses, and a few others started the cooking fires for supper and coffee. Guards were posted.

As Marcus and John sat near one of the fires and leaned back to look at the crackling flames, some of the men began singing an Irish ballad. The melody was hauntingly beautiful, but Marcus couldn't understand the words.

"What are they singing?" he asked Sergeant Flynn. "What is that language?"

"Sure an' that would be Gaelic now," Flynn said. "'Tis a song of the old sod."

"Sergeant, how long ago did you come from Ireland?" Marcus asked.

"'Twas a bit over six years ago, sir," Flynn said. "Was took right into the Union Army, I was, an' less'n two months after I arrived in America I found myself in the terrible Battle of Pittsburg's Landin'. Though I reckon most is callin' it Shiloh now."

"Your father was at Shiloh," Marcus said to John.

"On the opposite side from the good sergeant here, I'm afraid," John said.

"Sure'n at the time I had no side but me own," Flynn said. "No, an' neither did most of the laddies I knew. 'Twas hard for one from the old country to understand how folks could be killin' their own kind. Ever' man that died was speakin' the same tongue, an' there was Irish on both sides, too."

"But you stayed in the Army," Marcus said. "Aye, sir, I stayed in," Flynn said. He pointed to the others. "I'm just like them. The Army is home to us. We get our three squares an' a place to be with our own kind. 'Tis family an' church an' country, all rolled into one. The Army takes care of its own, Lieutenant, and we're its own. Just like you."

"Me?"

"Aye, sir, you. I know there's officers an' there's enlisted men, an' the two can't never be no friends or nothin' like that, but truth to tell, Lieutenant, we're all alike under this here blue tunic we're wearin'. Some of us are good, an' some are bad. Some are brave an' some are cowards. But we're all goin' to wind up in Fiddler's Green sooner or later."

"Fiddler's Green?" John said, confused by the term.

"Aye, Fiddler's Green. Sure an' don't be tellin' me you've no knowledge of Fiddler's Green?"

"I'm afraid I've never heard of it," John said.

"I would've thought that coming from a military family you'd know all about it," Marcus said.

"I wasn't around my father much during the war," John said. "And since the war he won't speak of anything military."

Marcus nodded. "Fiddler's Green is the place where all the old cavalrymen go when they die," Marcus explained. "It's a cool, shaded glen where the drinking is free, and every company who ever rode to a trumpet's call is there, waiting for that final roll call on Judgment Day."

John chuckled nervously. "You don't really believe that, do you? What about you, Sergeant Flynn, do you believe it?"

"Aye, sir, I believe it," Flynn answered. "And why not? If a body can believe in a heaven and a hell, then wouldn't you be thinkin' that the Lord would allow such a place to exist if all the souls of the soldiers wanted it to?"

"Well, when you put it like that . . ." John mused. "I suppose it is pleasant to think about, isn't it?"

"It has comforted many a trooper who's had to face the idea of dying in some deserted valley all alone," Flynn said. Flynn had been smoking a pipe, and now he knocked the bowl out into the fire. "If you've no objections, Lieutenant, I'll be checkin' the guard and then turnin' in. We'll be seein' some Indians tomorra."

"Tomorrow? What about tonight?" John asked.

"I don't think so, Lieutenant," Flynn replied. "Like as not they'll be dancin' all night to make their medicine. You see, they don't like fightin' at night. They'll do it if they have to, but the heathens believe a body that gets kilt in the night is doomed to spend eternity in darkness."

"Thank you, Sergeant," Marcus said. "Anyway, I'm glad there's not much chance of us being attacked tonight. With all these fresh recruits, it's going to be rough enough if they hit us tomorrow in the daytime."

"Don't be worryin' none about the recruits," Flynn said. "I've been with 'em for most of the month now, an' I think they'll do just fine when the time comes."

"Thanks, Sergeant," John said honestly.

When Flynn left to check on the guards, Marcus and John spread out their sleeping rolls. Marcus lay on his side, staring into the fire, which by now had burned so low that the flames were tiny blue flickers above the glowing red coals.

"Marcus," John called quietly from the dark.

"Yes?"

"Do you think we'll fight Indians tomorrow?"

"I don't know."

"You scared?"

"No," Marcus said, and even as he said the word he knew it was true.

"Me, neither," John said. "But I don't mind admitting I sort of wish we would get attacked. I'm anxious for some action."

"You heard what Flynn said. There will be action enough for everybody before this is all over."

"Yes, I guess that's true." There was a long, pregnant pause, then again, John's voice came through the dark.

"Did you write to my sister?"

"Yes, I did."

"Don't get me wrong," John said. "I only ask because I'm curious. It's not that I'm wanting to play the role of matchmaker or anything." John was quiet after that exchange, and for several moments there was no sound other than the popping of the fire, the yelp of a distant coyote, the whir of the night insects, and a guard's cough. Then, again, came John's quiet voice from the dark.

"Still, if something were to happen between the two of you, it would really be great, wouldn't it?"

"Good night, John," Marcus said, and turned over.

Marcus felt certain that even if they saw Indians, they wouldn't be attacked. Missouri Joe had told him that Indians only attacked if they were sure they had the advantage. He was leading a platoon of thirty privates, as well as three corporals, a sergeant, and another lieutenant besides himself. That was a total of thirty-six well-armed men. It would take a sizable war party to wage an attack against them.

The next morning, he told the men that though they might encounter Indians today, he didn't expect an attack. Nevertheless, he instructed them to check their weapons and to be sure in their minds how they would react in case the Indians did attack. Then they prepared food to be eaten in the saddle for the noon meal, and when all was ready, he signaled for the trumpeter to sound boots and saddles.

"Won't the Injuns hear the trumpet an' know where

we are and what we're doin', Lieutenant?" one of the men asked.

"I'm sure they will," Marcus said. "But would you have us sneak out of here like some whipped pups? Or leave proudly, like members of the United States Cavalry?"

"No, we're soldiers, by God!" one of the others shouted.

"Well, then, let's leave here like soldiers," Marcus suggested.

The company rode out in a column of twos. Within an hour every man among them knew that the Indians were indeed watching, for they could be seen as they rode single file along the crest of the hills. They were always keeping pace with the platoon and making no effort to hide themselves. But, as Marcus had figured, they made no move to attack, either. The Indians followed them to within two miles of Fort Reynolds, then they turned and rode away.

"You played it smart, Lieutenant," Flynn said as he watched them ride off. "There wasn't enough of 'em in their raidin' party, and they was afraid to take us on."

"D'ya hear that, boys?" one of the soldiers up front shouted back to the column. "They was afraid to take us on. They know better'n to mess with the men of the Fourth!"

"Yeah!" someone shouted, and another came out with a "Hurrah for the Fourth!" They followed that with hurrahs for Lieutenant Cavanaugh and for Lieutenant Culpepper.

A short time later they saw the stockade walls of Fort Reynolds.

"Sergeant, review the column, please, and make certain everyone is deporting themselves properly," Marcus ordered.

"Aye, sir, I'll see that the lads have a proper dress when we ride through the gates," Flynn said. He peeled his horse away from the head of the column and moved along the line of soldiers, his practiced eyes picking out an unbuttoned blouse here, a misfastened buckle there. Several times he made corrections in uniform, equipment, or even how the trooper was sitting his horse. Then, when he was satisfied that all were ready, he galloped back to the front.

"All ready, sir," Flynn said, falling in alongside Culpepper.

"Thank you, Sergeant," Marcus said. "We may have left with a platoon of raw recruits, but I feel that we're bringing back soldiers."

"Aye, sir, my feelin' exactly," Sergeant Flynn said.

As they had when the company left three days ago, the fort's compliment was turned out for their return. All the companies were lined up in parade formation, and the officers were again standing in review at the sally port. Marcus could see Colonel Pettibone mounted just in front of the flagpole. The band began playing as the men came through the gate.

"Look sharp, men!" Marcus called, and he could see them sitting tall in their saddles, their chests swelled out, their faces filled with pride. True, the Indians had not engaged them in battle, but a group of untried soldiers had conducted a well-disciplined sweep through hostile land. The men had every right to hold up their heads.

And so did he.

He wheeled right, then made square around the quadrangle. When he approached Colonel Pettibone, he ordered, "Eyes right!" and as the left column turned their eyes toward Colonel Pettibone, and the right column stared straight ahead, Marcus and John rendered salutes with their sabers.

- It was a magnificent moment.

5

IN CELEBRATION OF THE COMPLETION OF TRAINING FOR the new platoon, it was customary to put the rigors of drill and patrolling behind them at a party sponsored by the company that would be receiving the new men. In this case it was D Company, commanded by Captain Forsyth. All the officers of the entire regiment, as well as the non-commissioned officers and men of D Company, were in attendance.

The recruits were dressed for the first time in their full-dress uniforms, and they stood in awkward groups on either side of the dance floor at the sutler's store, feeling a sheepish pride over the gold buttons and braid and yellow flash that marked them at last as Cavalry troopers. The women, resplendent in fancy gowns, saucy curls, and flashing ear-bobs, whirled across the dance floor with first one partner, then another.

It wasn't until such moments that the disparity

between the numbers of men and women was noticeable. Only six of the twenty officers and nine of the thirty sergeants had wives. There were six laundresses who were unmarried, making a total of twenty-one women. That was the total number of women on the whole post and had the entire regiment turned out for the dance, the women would have been lost in the crowd.

According to regulations, D Company was supposed to have 78 privates, a wagoner, a saddler, 2 farriers, 2 trumpeters, 8 corporals, 5 sergeants, a second lieutenant, a first lieutenant, and a captain. Like most of the Army units out West, however, they were understrength and, even with the addition of 30 new recruits, still had but 60 enlisted men. John Culpepper filled the second lieutenant's slot while Marcus, though only a second lieutenant, occupied the position of first lieutenant and executive officer.

At such dances there was no jealousy evidenced by husbands as they generously allowed their wives' dance cards to be filled. Though the women seemed to enjoy such parties, they found that every moment of their evening was taken.

Marcus danced dutifully with Martha Pettibone and Janet Forsyth, the wives of his regimental and company commanders. Martha, as befitting a colonel's wife, was a bit stiff and formal, but Janet seemed to genuinely enjoy the party. She was a good dancer and seemed as at ease with the enlisted men as she was with the officers.

Ironically, Marcus found Drusilla Conklin to be the most interesting. Though he had only seen her in the shadow of her husband's alcoholism before now, she seemed to shine at the dance. She was an excellent dancer and, during their dance, they got engaged in a conversation about the work of the Dutch artist, Jan Vermeer. Marcus was an amateur artist himself, and Vermeer was his favorite. He was delighted at how much Drusilla Conklin knew about his work, and she seemed equally delighted to have found someone who could discuss what was obviously her own secret passion.

After a few dances, the band played a fanfare, and Colonel Pettibone stepped in front of them and held out his arms, calling for quiet. He was smiling broadly, good-naturedly, and Marcus realized that Pettibone was in his glory at such functions. Some men were meant to be bankers or lawyers or tradesmen. Pettibone's destiny was to be a solider. Marcus felt that about himself as well.

"Would you be givin' us a speech now, Colonel?" one of the sergeants called.

"Well, that's just what I'm going to do if you'll be quiet and allow it," Pettibone said, and the men laughed.

"Ladies, officers, men. I want to welcome our new recruits . . . and our new officers," he added, including Marcus and John, though Marcus had already been here for three and a half months, "to the Fourth

Cavalry . . . the finest fighting outfit ever to wear the uniform of the United States Army!"

"Hurrah!" the men shouted and stamped noisily on the floor until Pettibone quieted them again.

"And now I can tell you that what we have been waiting for has come through. This afternoon I received a dispatch from General Sheridan, authorizing the Fourth Cavalry to conduct an extended scout against Two Eagles. Enjoy yourselves tonight, men, for tomorrow we go on the hunt."

"Hurrah, hurrah!" The men shouted and whistled, and there was a buzz of excitement as they started talking among themselves.

"Bandmaster resume the dance," Pettibone said, his eyes shining brightly.

Marcus tried to remain calm on the outside, but he was as excited as the men were over the prospect of seeing some real action.

They had been on patrol for five days, but so far their search had been fruitless. Twice they had seen small, mounted bands of warriors, but the warriors were traveling light on fast ponies and they easily outdistanced the soldiers, then returned to laugh and mock them. It was a very frustrating expedition for the men.

Then, on the afternoon of the fifth day, Missouri Joe found signs that they may be close to a large party. Pettibone halted his company and made camp, while a patrol of six went out looking. Marcus, to his delight, was given command of the patrol.

"Now remember," Captain Forsyth said as he gave Marcus his instructions. "You aren't to engage them, you are just to find them, then report back to us."

"Yes, sir," Marcus said.

Marcus ordered the men to strip themselves and their horses of anything that might rattle, jangle, or clank.

"I want us to be able to ride fast and silent," he explained.

Marcus chose Sergeant Flynn to go along as his second-in-command. William Shield was one of the other men in his patrol.

Marcus and his men followed the river for about an hour. Finally they stopped to water their horses, and when they did, Marcus saw something, or thought he saw something, moving on the hills above them. He looked again, but there was nothing there.

"What is it, Lieutenant?" Flynn asked. "Did you see something?"

"I don't know," Marcus admitted. "I thought I did, but when I looked again, there was nothing there."

"Aye, sir, an' that's the way of it," Flynn said. "When one of us that's been around a wee while says we see Indians, most of the time we don't really see 'em. We just sorta feel 'em. And I been feelin' 'em for 'bout the last half hour or so."

Marcus took off his hat and brushed his hair back. "I wish we could actually see them. I'd like to have something definite to report to Colonel Pettibone when..."

Suddenly there was the singing *swoosh* of an arrow, and it made a hollow sound as it hit Marcus's saddle. The arrow stuck, and the shaft quivered right in front of Marcus's leg. Marcus looked at it in surprise, struck dumb for just an instant by the shock of the near miss. His horse jumped once nervously, through it had not actually been hit.

"There they are!" Flynn shouted, and he pointed to a hill about one hundred yards away. A band of Cheyenne came pouring over the top of the hill, swooping down at them, whooping and shouting at the top of their lungs. Marcus didn't take time to count them, but he estimated that there were about thirty braves in the band.

"Let's get out of here!" Marcus shouted, and he slapped his heels against the flank of his horse, urging him on. As they raced away, they stayed close along the bank of the river, occasionally slipping down into the water itself to send up sheets of spray.

Marcus was in complete control of his animal, and he knew that he could get much more speed if he needed it. But he held his mount in check to stay back with the others. He looked back over his shoulder and saw that the Indians were gaining on them. They were so close that they couldn't miss if they shot at them, and Marcus wondered why they weren't firing.

Marcus pulled his pistol and twisted around in the saddle to aim toward the Indians.

"No, Lieutenant, don't shoot at 'em!" Flynn shouted.

"Why the hell shouldn't I?" Marcus shouted back.

"They ain't shot us yet, 'cause they want to take coups," Flynn explained. "But if we shoot first, they'll shoot back, an' with that many of 'em this close, they won't miss."

Suddenly Marcus saw Captain Forsyth and the entire D Company coming over the hill just ahead of them.

"Look!" Marcus shouted. "This way, men! Head for Captain Forsyth!"

Marcus and the others left the riverbank and started toward Captain Forsyth. The Indians, seeing the other soldiers for the first time, drew their horses up and stopped. They wheeled about in confusion and started to retreat. Marcus saw them turning and stopped.

"Now!" he shouted. "Let's go get them!" Marcus now began urging the horse on faster and faster, getting everything out of the animal that he could. He closed ground rapidly, though at the same time he was pulling away from his own companions. Within a short time he had drawn even with the rear ranks of the Indians.

Outnumbered by the Cavalry, the Indians were fleeing and fighting for their lives. Those who had rifles turned them toward Marcus and fired.

Marcus heard and felt the angry buzz of half a dozen bullets going by him. He pulled his pistol and returned their fire, though his shooting proved equally ineffective.

Marcus saw an Indian with a red blanket carrying a

lance. At the end of the lance dangled a tuft of yellow hair, and he realized it had to be a white scalp. He thought of the wagon he had found, with the slain mother and daughter and the mutilated father. He took slow, deliberate aim, fired, and had the satisfaction of seeing the Indian tumble from his saddle. He had no time to enjoy it, though, because at that very moment he was struck and unseated by a thrown war club. He hit the ground with a bone-jarring thud, rolled and tumbled painfully across the rocks, and finally came to a stop. He raised himself up to see the Indians scattering into every direction like a covey of flushed quail, just as the advance elements of the Cavalry pounded by in hot pursuit.

"Go!" Marcus screamed loudly, forgetting the pain of his fall in the excitement of the moment. "Go! Get 'em!"

Marcus watched the soldiers who had been behind pass him by. It was like having a box seat at a thrilling sports event. The horses were magnificent with their nostrils flared, their teeth bared, their manes flying, and their muscles working in powerful coordination. The riders were bending low over the animals' necks, the brim of their service hats rolled back by the breeze, their eyes narrowed, their faces tautly set. It was a full-blown Cavalry charge—and his first victory.

With the horses secured and the guards posted, the officers gathered around the campfire that night. In addition to providing a fire for cooking and making coffee, the fires provided much-needed warmth, for the nights were beginning to get very cool. Winter wasn't too far away . . . the leaves were changing colors, and several times over the last few days he had seen geese flying south, etching dark Vs high against the crystal blue sky.

"Good work out there today, Cavanaugh," Pettibone said to Marcus as he took a drink of his coffee.

"Thank you, sir. It was a successful strategy," Marcus said. "The only question I have is why you didn't tell me what my real purpose was to be."

"I wasn't sure how you would act if you knew what I had in mind," Pettibone said. "Colonel, I know my duty."

"It isn't that, Cavanaugh," Conklin said. "It's just that you were bait for the trap. And in case you haven't noticed, most of the time when bait is used to set a trap . . . the creature being trapped gets the bait."

Conklin was sober tonight, one of the few times Marcus had seen him that way. He was staying sober with an effort. "I know a little about being the bait in a trap," he said as he poured himself a fourth cup of coffee.

"What do you mean, sir?" Marcus asked.

"I was with the First Maine outside Petersburg," Conklin said. "In what they called 'ten minutes of hell.'"

"Yes, sir. I've heard about the battle."

The First Maine was sent in advance of the real charge in order to get the Confederates to commit themselves. Nine hundred men started the attack; within ten minutes, 632 lay dead or wounded, including sixty-five percent of the officers. In one battalion, no one higher than the rank of sergeant was left alive.

"Then you can understand when I say I know a little something about baiting a trap," Conklin said. "Takes a toll on a man. . . ." Marcus knew that Conklin was referring to his drinking problem, but he didn't comment on it. It was an embarrassing moment and he knew that Conklin already regretted it. A few of the officers around the fire cleared their throats nervously, then someone began reliving the day's action, and the moment passed.

"Eleven of them, by God. We got eleven of the heathen bastards," one of the officers said.

"I wonder if Two Eagles was with them?"

"No, he wasn't," Missouri Joe said. He had been out in the dark and he now walked into the golden bubble of light that spread out from the fire. No one offered him a cup of coffee, and he didn't ask for one. Instead, he cut off a plug from his chewing tobacco and stuck it in his mouth. "The leader of that there bunch was Standing Horse. He mostly operates up around the Bighorn Mountains."

"Isn't this a little far away for someone like that to be operating?" Forsyth asked.

"Yep," Missouri Joe answered. "And the funny thing is, some of Two Eagles's bucks was ridin' with 'em. That don't normally happen 'less there's somethin' up. Iffen you was to ask me, I say there's a real gatherin' takin' place."

"Why do you think that is?" Marcus asked.

By now, Missouri Joe had a big quid of tobacco worked up, and he squirted some juice toward the fire. It sizzled as it hit a hot coal.

"Oh, hell, boy, I don't have to reckon what it is. I know what it is. They're gatherin' up to make war."

"On us?" Marcus asked.

Missouri Joe spit again, then wiped the back of his hand across his mouth and beard. "Well now, boy, iffen by 'us' you mean all the white folks that's settlin' this country, then I'd have to say yeah. They're hopin' to run ever' last one of you out."

Joe squatted down Indian style next to the fire.

"'Course I ain't includin' myself. I done married up with a Indian woman. The Indians is more acceptin' than the whites. Moon Cow Woman sure ain't looked on by other whites as one of them 'cause she's my wife, but me bein' the husband of Moon Cow Woman is another thing. They ain't a Indian village between the Missouri and the Canadian border that I can't go into."

"Including Two Eagles's village?" Pettibone said.

"Well, sir, I tell you . . ." Missouri Joe said. He took out his chewing tobacco and cut off another plug, then stuck it in his mouth before he spoke again. "The truth is, Indians is funny about that, too. I could go into his village, sure enough, and I'd be welcome around the fires. That is, long as I was to go in friendly-like. But iffen I was to come ridin' in with a bunch of soldier boys, they'd be shootin' at me just like they would you."

"It makes me wonder," Pettibone mused, "if in fact you would be shooting back at them?"

"I don't take your meaning, Colonel," Missouri Joe said.

"I mean, in such a case, just where would your loyalties lie?"

Missouri Joe squinted across at Pettibone for a long, silent moment, then he stood up and sent another squirt of tobacco quid and juice into the fire. "I reckon I'll go take a look at the horses," he said, making no response to Pettibone's question.

"Colonel Pettibone, sir, you had no call to question his loyalty like that," Forsyth said.

"The man is an Indian lover," Pettibone said. "You heard him talking, how when the Indians went on the warpath they wouldn't go against him."

"Unless he was leading us right into their war camp," Forsyth said. "The fact that he's willing to do that when he would otherwise be in no danger from them is all the proof I need of his loyalty."

"Yes, well, perhaps some of us are more easily bamboozled than others, Captain," Pettibone replied.

"Did I ever tell you about the time we were down on the Republican and Captain Peters from the Fifth . . .," one of the other officers started after the awkward silence.

With the immediate tension eased, Marcus stood up and walked away from the fire. He wandered through the camp for a few moments, looking and listening to the men of the 4th . . . storytelling here, laughter over there, and the inevitable singing. Soon he found himself close to the remuda where the bodies of the eleven Indians who had been killed today were laid out in a line. He walked down the row of bodies until he came to the one he had killed . . . the tall one who had been carrying the lance with the blond scalp. There was a small, blue bullet hole in his chest, just over the heart. It had only taken one shot to kill him instantly.

The Indian's eyes were open, though one of them was half-closed. As Marcus stared down at him it gave him a disquieting feeling, as if the Indian he had killed was staring back.

"His name is Dog Runner," a voice said from the dark behind him.

"What?" Marcus turned around quickly and saw Missouri Joe coming toward him.

"That tall fella layin' there," Missouri Joe said. "His name is Dog Runner. Indians, you know, got a way about names. They got to mean somethin'. Now, Dog Runner here, when he was just a young buck, all full of piss and vinegar, made a bet that he could run faster'n any dog in the camp. 'Course he couldn't, but the fact that he was foolish enough to think that he could, give him his name, an' it stuck with him for the rest of his life. He's the one you kilt, ain't he?"

"Yes," Marcus said. Morbidly, his eyes were drawn back to stare at Dog Runner. "Yes, he is. I didn't know you knew him."

"Oh, yeah, I been knowin' him a long time. He's my wife's cousin."

"Oh. I ... I'm sorry."

Missouri chuckled. "What are you sorry about, boy? Are you sorry that you kilt him? Or are you sorry that I know him?"

"I'm sorry that he's your relative," Marcus said.

Missouri Joe pulled out a plug of tobacco and carved off a piece, offered it to Marcus who declined, then put it away.

"Hell, I ain't sorry that you kilt him," Missouri Joe said.

"Why would you say a thing like that?" "Boy, let me tell you somethin' else about Dog Runner. He was as mean as they come. Three winters ago he let his mother-in-law starve to death 'cause he wouldn't take no responsibility for her. He wasn't put down none by the other Indians for that, 'cause they figure it's pretty much live and let live as far as a person's own family is concerned. He beat his woman an' kids, too, but it won't do no good to stand here spoutin' off all the evil things about Dog Runner. He wasn't much of a man in my book, and if there ever was somebody that needed killin', why, I reckon it was ol' Dog Runner here. He ain't gonna be missed much back in his village—especially not by his woman and his kids. But that ain't the point I'm trying to make here, Lieutenant."

Marcus looked up at him.

"The point I'm tryin' to make here is, they's some folks need killin' be they white or red. But them's that need it, need it for what kind of men they be, and not just 'cause they happen to be Indian. Do you get what I'm sayin', Lieutenant?"

"Yes, I do," Marcus said.

"The thing is, you a brand-new shavetail. I figure you got twenty, maybe thirty years in front of you. You probably gonna have the chance to kill lots of Indians in that time. You not gonna always know that they was once dumb enough to think they could run faster'n any dog in camp, or mean enough to let their mother-in-law starve. But they are men. Men, Lieutenant . . . not heathens or animals or targets. They're men, an' some of 'em's good and some 'em's bad. 'Member that, son."

"I'll remember, Joe," Marcus promised. "I'll remember."

6

THEY HAD BEEN ON THE TRAIL FOR HALF THE MORNING the next day when Missouri Joe came across Indian signs indicating a hundred or more horses, plus the tracks of dozens of travois. He pointed it out to Colonel Pettibone, and the regimental commander halted the march, then immediately ordered his trumpeter to sound officers' call.

The shrill summons of the trumpet carried back along the column to D Company, where Captain Forsyth twisted around in his saddle and looked at his two lieutenants to see if they'd heard it. Their curious and anxious expressions told him that they did.

"First Sergeant!" Forsyth bellowed, and the first sergeant rode up to the head of D Company's column. "Take over."

"Aye, sir," the first sergeant responded. He stood in his stirrups and looked back over the entire company.

"At my command," he shouted, indicating that he was now in charge of the troop.

Because Army regulations for mounted and dismounted drill and ceremony state that an officer is never a part of a formation commanded by an enlisted man, both Marcus and John fell out of ranks immediately—no specific order was necessary—and moved up alongside Forsyth. The three officers then urged their horses into a canter, hurrying them to the front of the halted regiment, where all the other officers of the 4th were also gathering.

Pettibone was sitting casually in his saddle with one leg hooked across the pommel. He was distractedly tapping that leg with his riding quirt and he smiled broadly at his officers.

"Well, gentlemen, it would appear this is our day," he said. "Do you see this?" He pointed to the ground behind him where the Indian trail could be easily seen, not only by the broken and chewed grass, but by the line of horse droppings. "The hostiles have made it easy for us. They have practically sent us an open invitation."

Missouri Joe, who was present for the meeting, leaned over to spit.

"Colonel, don't that worry you just a mite?" he asked. "I mean, that it all seems so easy?" Pettibone turned to look at his civilian scout. "What are you suggesting?" he asked.

"Well, I'm just thinkin' that we ain't exactly sneakin' up on 'em. Since they're movin' their whole camp . . .

women, children, dogs, an' ever'thin', it don't hardly seem right they'd make it so easy for us."

"Well, Mr. Indian Scout, have you considered the fact that they may have no choice?" "I ain't followin' you, Colonel."

"I mean, even Indian horses have to eat," Pettibone said. "And what goes in at the front of the horse, comes out at the rear." Pettibone pointed again to the trail. "Unless they have their squaws following behind picking up turds, they are going to be easy to follow." Several of the officers laughed at the mental image of a group of Indian women walking along behind the horses, picking up the horses' droppings. Missouri Joe, without laughing, leaned forward and spit again.

"Well, Colonel, now you're gettin' smart," he said. "You see, I seen the squaws and young'uns do just that."

"Obviously, they haven't done it this time," Pettibone said, "for anyone can plainly see that 'Lo' is just in front of us." "Lo" was often used as a sarcastic name for the Indians. It referred to the author James Fenimore Cooper's line, "Lo, the noble red man."

"What are we going to do, Colonel?" one of the officers asked.

"Here is my plan," Pettibone replied. "I'm going to form two squadrons of two companies each. Captain Andrews, you will take your company and B Company from First Battalion, and form a squadron that will go south for one mile, then ride west, parallel with the line of march. Major Conklin, you will take the remaining company from First Battalion, and one company from

Second Battalion to form a squadron that will parallel the route of march on the north. That will leave two companies of the Second Battalion, which, when joined to the three of the Third Battalion, will form a strengthened squadron for the attack. This reinforced squadron will proceed right up the middle of the Indian trail until we encounter the savages. And then, gentlemen, we will attack, leaving the squadrons on each wing in position to cut off any possible retreat. Captain Forsyth, you will command the attack squadron."

"Yes, sir," Forsyth said.

Marcus felt a sense of excitement at being part of the center squadron, the squadron that would actually make the attack. That excitement was short-lived, however, for Colonel Pettibone continued with his instructions. "I shall establish a regimental headquarters to direct the operation, and I want two officers to join my staff—Lieutenants Cavanaugh and Humes."

Marcus took a quick breath, ready to protest. He realized, however, that any protest would not only be futile, but would mark him as someone who questioned command. He was disappointed, but he held his disappointment in check.

"Colonel, shall we agree upon some signal for assistance?" Andrews asked.

Pettibone chuckled. "I scarcely think that will be the problem," he said. "No, sir, the problem will be as it always is . . . preventing these pesky savages from running away." Pettibone pulled out his watch and looked at it. "It is now nine-thirty. I propose to make the attack by ten o'clock. I expect all of you to be in position by that time."

Marcus could sense that Pettibone was smelling battle now and, like a predator on the scent of blood, could scarcely wait until the battle was joined.

Forsyth, Conklin, and Captain Andrews set their watches to coincide with Pettibone's.

"You remaining company commanders will take your commands from your respective squadron leader. All right, gentlemen, return to your men. Lieutenants Cavanaugh and Humes, stay with me."

As Marcus watched Captain Forsyth and Lieutenant Culpepper canter back to the company, he couldn't help but feel a bit jealous. Though Culpepper was trying very hard to hide it, Marcus could see that a broad smile of excitement was on the young lieutenant's face.

John was going to be in on the attack, Marcus was going to merely observe it.

A few moments later Captain Andrews's squadron pulled away to the south, while major Conklin's squadron pulled away to the north. Lieutenant Cavanaugh, with the center squadron, continued right up the path of broken and chewed grass and brown-and- green horse apples. The headquarters staff followed, but from the rear.

"Well, Lieutenant Cavanaugh, what do you think of my plan of battle?" Pettibone asked.

The query surprised Marcus. He wondered why

Pettibone would ask him such a question. "You're asking me, sir?"

"Yes. you're the most recent graduate of the academy . . . you've studied tactics since any of the rest of us have. What do you think?" "The only fault I see with your battle plan is that I was pulled away from the squadron that is making the attack, sir," he said.

Pettibone laughed. "Well said, Mr. Cavanaugh, well said. However, don't be feeling too much despair. I'm certain you will see your share of battle before this is all through." "Yes, sir," Marcus said.

A few moments later they stopped while Pettibone stared through his glasses. "Damn!" he said aloud. "Missouri Joe was right. The Indians are leading us astray. But how the hell did they get over there?"

"I beg your pardon, sir?"

Pettibone pointed, and then, for the first time, Marcus saw a cloud of dust in the distance, north of the direction they were traveling. He was angry with himself for not having seen it before, because it was a fairly large cloud and clearly visible.

"It would seem, Mr. Cavanaugh, that the Indians have left us a broad highway to travel while they have positioned themselves for an attack at my flank. Captain Andrews is about to be engaged. Lieutenant Humes."

"Yes, sir?"

"Go to Major Conklin, tell him to circle around to prevent any attempt by the Indians to escape. Lieutenant Cavanaugh, I want you to overtake Captain

Andrews. Tell him that I will send Conklin around to cut off any possible retreat, and instruct Forsyth to support him in the attack. He is to strike the enemy at once with everything he has. Do you have that? He should hit them with everything he has."

"Yes, sir. Colonel?"

"Yes, what is it?"

"Request permission to stay with the captain during the fighting, sir."

"Permission granted," Pettibone said. "Now get going, Lieutenant!"

Marcus spurred his mount into a gallop and bent low over the horse's neck. He could hear the animal's labored breathing and the pounding of its hooves, but nothing seemed louder than the beating of his own heart. The ground before him descended in a long, gradual slope that was covered with tall, dry grass. It made riding easy, and a short time later he pulled up at the head of Captain Andrews's column.

"Has the colonel seen them?" Andrews asked, indicating the Indians in front of them.

"Yes, sir, he has," Marcus replied breathlessly. "Colonel Pettibone's compliments, sir, and he asks that you strike against the Cheyenne from the front, as soon as you can engage them, with everything you have."

"A frontal assault?" Andrews questioned. "Is Colonel Pettibone fully aware of the number of hostiles there? A frontal assault would be a massacre!"

Marcus was a little surprised by Andrews's

response. As the commander in the field had ordered a frontal assault.

There should be no discussion. Colonel Pettibone would be proceeding upon the assumption that Andrews's response would be immediate unquestioned obedience to his orders. For a commander in battle there could be no other way ... it was the cardinal precept of military command. And yet Andrews was questioning Pettibone's orders, even as Marcus was transmitting them.

"Sir, I would strongly recommend that you proceed as directed," Marcus said.

"Will he be holding a squadron in reserve?" "No, sir," Marcus said. "Major Conklin's squadron is being moved into position to block the Indians' retreat, Captain Forsyth's squadron is coming to your support."

"I see," Andrews said. "Well, Lieutenant, here is where you get an example of contingency battlefield strategy. First I shall attack with one company. Then, while they have the Indians engaged, the second company will strike in a classic Cavalry charge. That should break up the hostiles, and the field will be ours."

"Captain, perhaps I do not interpret Colonel Pettibone's orders as you have, but I believe when he says strike with everything, he means exactly that."

"I submit, sir, that you are merely to transmit the commander's orders, not to interpret them," Andrews said.

"Yes, sir," Marcus replied. He was silent then. To say anything else would be tantamount to insubordination.

"Captain, I've received permission from Colonel Pettibone to accompany you into battle . . . with your approval, of course." Andrews smiled. "I would be pleased to have you," he said. "You may join A Company. They will engage first."

"Thank you, sir," Marcus said.

Andrews called his company commanders over and issued his orders to them. "Varney, Lieutenant Cavanaugh will go with you." "Right," Lieutenant Varney said. "Come along now, Lieutenant. Let's give these heathens a run for their money."

Marcus followed Varney back to his company, where orders were given to form in a company front skirmish line.

"Lieutenant Cavanaugh, you take the left side, I'll take the right," Varney said. "If I go down, you're in command."

"Yes, sir," Marcus said. He smiled. "Lieutenant Varney?"

"Yes."

"I don't have that much ambition. Watch out for yourself."

"Right," Varney said, smiling back at Marcus.

Marcus hurried over to get into position, then turned and watched as the company formed into a long line abreast.

"Draw carbines!" the first sergeant shouted, and the men pulled their weapons from their saddle scabbards. The horses seemed to sense the impending danger, perhaps from the men atop them, and grew a bit skittish. A couple of horses began nervously prancing around, moving out of the line, and the riders had to turn them in a full circle to get them back into position.

Marcus looked over at Varney and saw that the lieutenant had his saber drawn. Marcus drew his own, then rested his hand on his saddle horn. He looked down and saw that he was shaking. Was it fear or excitement? Marcus didn't want to admit that it was fear, but he realized that it was probably a little of both.

"Forward at a trot!" Varney shouted, and the company started out across the plains.

As they rode toward the cloud of dust, they were soon able to see the figures within it. The Indians weren't retreating. They were advancing slowly, yet confidently, ready to take on the white man and defeat him.

In this engagement the Cheyenne outnumbered not only Varney's single company but Captain Andrews's entire squadron. In a classic tactical maneuver that Marcus might have studied in the classroom, the Indians had managed to position themselves in such a way as to enjoy a numerical superiority on the field, even though the overall numbers favored the enemy.

"Trumpeter! Sound the charge!" Varney called.

The trumpeter lifted his instrument, and the thrilling notes of the mounted charge carried like a clarion call above the jangle of equipment and the sounds of the horses.

With the charge sounded, the company surged

forward at top speed, and soon the sound of galloping horses' hooves was like thunder rolling across the plains. Above all the noise, the soldiers could clearly hear the Indians as they whooped and shouted in anticipation of battle. They hurtled toward one another. Two armies: one uniformed, structured and trained; the other half-naked and swarming, but no less determined.

Marcus slashed at the first warrior with his saber but the red man leaned deftly to one side and the blade flashed by harmlessly, even as the Indian struck out at Marcus with his war club, also missing his target. Now their momentum carried them on to other targets.

"Use your pistol, lad!" one of the older veteran privates shouted to Marcus. "That saber is as worthless as tits on a boar hog!"

Though the private's remarks could have been considered insubordinate, Marcus knew he was right. He drew his pistol with his free hand as another Indian was charging toward him, screaming and holding his war club over his head. Marcus quickly took aim, amazed at how calmly he was able to sit in his saddle and wait, and when his attacker was almost upon him, he pulled the trigger. The gun jumped in his hand, and a bio hole suddenly appeared in the Indian's chest. There was a look of surprise on the brave's face as he pitched backward out of his saddle.

Suddenly Marcus heard a whistling sound, then a thud, and he saw the arrow buried deep in his horse's neck. The horse went down, and Marcus was thrown over its head, rolling as he hit the ground. As he got to his feet, another Indian rode up and, holding his rifle with one hand, fired at Marcus. The bullet passed so close by his head that Marcus could feel the breeze it created. He immediately took aim with his pistol, firing off a perfect head shot, killing the Cheyenne brave instantly.

A riderless Cavalry horse ran by then, and Marcus managed to reach out and grab the animal's halter. The horse fell to its front knees and slid along the ground for a few feet, stunned by the sudden grab. Marcus waited until the animal had regained its footing, then swung into the saddle, ready to continue the fight.

The sound of a single trumpet blowing charge cut through the noise, then a second joined in, then a third. The Cheyenne, realizing that they were soon to be outnumbered on the field, began to retreat. Andrews and his reserves, who were just now coming into the fray, were unable to stop them. His company and what was left of Varney's A Company started after the fleeing Indians, but the warriors had broken up into dozens of small groups and were pulling steadily away.

The Cavalry chased them for a few minutes, then Andrews held up his hand and brought them to a halt.

"All right, men, let's return to the scene of the battle," he said. "We have our wounded to consider."

Marcus and the others rode back at a trot, and when they reached the battlefield, Marcus saw that Pettibone and the other two squadrons had arrived. The wounded had been laid out on stretchers and were being attended to. Marcus swung down from his horse in front of Pettibone to report to him, but before he could say a word, Pettibone bristled in anger.

"If Andrews had hit them with everything he had, he would have been able to keep the Indians engaged until we arrived, and they wouldn't have gotten away. Lieutenant, what order did you transmit to Captain Andrews?" "I told him you wished him to strike from the front as soon as possible, and with everything he had."

"You did not suggest that I wanted him to hold part of his squadron back in reserve?" "No, sir, I did not," Marcus said.

"Very well, Lieutenant. Thank you," Pettibone said.

Marcus saw a line of canvas lumps lying nearby, with a handful of soldiers standing beside them. He knew that under the canvas lumps must be the bodies of cavalrymen, one of them, perhaps, the original rider of the horse that had fortuitously run by him on the battlefield.

"We lost nine men," Pettibone said, noticing the direction of Marcus's gaze. "Nine good men." He looked over toward Captain Andrews. "All because one of my officers failed to act upon the orders I gave him," he added in a quiet, angry voice.

At that moment Captain Forsyth approached, and Pettibone turned to him. "Captain, what's the count on hostiles? How many did we kill?"

"Fourteen," Captain Forsyth said. "Fourteen," Pettibone repeated. "Fourteen today and eleven yesterday, twenty-five in all." He nodded. "I would say then, Captain, that this has been a successful patrol. Call in the scouts. We are heading back to Fort Reynolds."

Shortly after the regiment returned to the post, Colonel Pettibone journeyed to Fort Wallace to report the results of his days in the field, and also to suggest that there was evidence of a major Indian gathering, perhaps a prelude to a major war.

Pettibone was gone for an entire week, and in his absence, command of the 4th Cavalry Regiment and Fort Reynolds fell to Major Conklin. However, as soon as the regiment was once more in garrison, Major Conklin slipped back into his alcoholic stupor. As a result, Captain Forsyth had to assume the duties of regimental commander, and that left Marcus as the acting commander of D Company.

It was just before evening retreat, when the sentry on the east wall reported a party of soldiers approaching. Everyone on the post knew that Colonel Pettibone was back.

They were already preparing to stand the retreat ceremony of lowering the flag at sunset. It was a very special formation, observed on every Army post and on board every Naval vessel.

Forsyth hurried over to meet the colonel to see if Colonel Pettibone intended to take the formation. The men watched anxiously, for if Pettibone took it, they knew they would have to go back to the stable and saddle their horses for mounted drill. To their relief, however, Forsyth returned and informed the officers that Colonel Pettibone would not resume command until tomorrow morning.

The regiment had been able to see everything because they were in company front formation on the parade ground. The officers and sergeants of each individual company had already seen to it that their men were in proper uniform, properly equipped, and in the correct formation. Now the soldiers were standing at ease, which meant they could talk quietly among themselves. Marcus could hear in the buzz of their conversation that they were glad "Spit 'n Polish" Pettibone was not going to take the formation. Marcus pretended he didn't hear them, for it wouldn't do for him to imply that he shared their opinions of the commanding officer.

"Lieutenant Cavanaugh?" Forsyth called quietly. Forsyth was standing at the head of the entire regimental formation and, like the men, in the at-ease position waiting for the signal cannon to indicate the exact time to strike the colors. With Forsyth acting as the regimental commander, the three battalions were being commanded by captains, while the companies were being handled by lieutenants. Marcus, however, was the only second lieutenant who was acting as a company commander.

"Yes, sir?"

"Colonel Pettibone has asked that I extend an invitation to you and Lieutenant Culpepper to have dinner with him this evening. Mrs. Forsyth and I will be going as well."

"I would be happy to attend, sir. I'll pass the invitation along to Lieutenant Culpepper."

"Very good. Stop by my house and we can go together."

"Yes, sir," Marcus answered.

At that moment the signal cannon boomed, and all conversation and restlessness came to a halt. Captain Forsyth came to attention, then addressed the formation.

"Commanders, bring your battalions to attention," he ordered.

Commands and supplementary commands echoed across the quadrangle.

"Battalion!" the battalion commanders shouted.

"Company!" the company commanders called.

"Platoon!" the platoon leaders added.

"Atten-hut!"

There was a rhythmic movement of the men coming to attention.

"Present!" Forsyth called.

"Present!" the supplementary commands rang out.

"Arms!" Forsyth barked.

There was no supplementary to the command of execution, and as one, the men's carbines and officers' sabers were raised in salute.

The trumpeter began playing retreat. As he played, the flag was lowered. All over the entire post, soldiers who were not in formation for one reason or another turned to salute the flag as it was being lowered. All civilians on the fort, from the laundresses on Soapsuds

Row, to the children and wives of the soldiers, to the sutler and his clerks, and even casual visitors, were expected to turn toward the flag and stand in respectful silence until the ceremony was over.

When the last note was but an echo, Captain Forsyth turned to face the formation.

"Dismiss the regiment," he called.

The subordinate commanders gave the necessary order, and one minute later the entire regiment, with the exception of those who were on additional duty, were free until six A.M. the following morning. Several soldiers started immediately for the sutler, where, already, beers were being filled and lined up on the bar for the expected onslaught.

7

When he came into Marcus Cavanaugh's quarters a little later that evening, John Culpepper was already dressed for dinner with the Colonel. Marcus was not ready and was standing over the chifforobe, pouring water into a wash basin. His shirt was off and his yellow galluses hung down to each side of his blue trousers, forming a yellow loop with the broad, yellow stripe down the sides of his legs. His pants were stuffed into high, well-polished boots. His tunic, with the empty golden shoulder boards denoting second lieutenant, was hanging over the back of a chair.

"Hello, John," Marcus said. He stropped his straight razor against a wide, leather strap. "I'll be ready in a few minutes. I thought I'd shave again before dinner with the brass."

"I stopped by the orderly room on the way over."

John held up a small, white envelope. "You have a letter here from Sally." He was smiling broadly.

"Do I, now?" Marcus answered.

"Aren't you going to read it?"

"Later."

"I thought you might want to read it now." Marcus looked over at his friend and smiled. "John, for someone who has no interest in playing the matchmaker, you seem pretty anxious to stir the pot."

"No, not really. I'm just curious, that's all," John defended.

"You know what they say about curiosity and the cat," Marcus teased. He lathered his face, then, drawing his jaw tight with the forefinger of his left hand, began pulling the razor through the soap. "Put it there on the table, I'll read it tonight before I go to bed."

"All right," John said, clearly disappointed that Marcus wasn't going to read it now and share it with him.

"Have a seat," Marcus invited. "I'll be ready in a few minutes, then we can walk over to Captain Forsyth's house together."

"All right," John said. "You got a new *Harper's Weekly*, too. I'll just have a look at it, if you don't mind."

"Go right ahead."

Marcus finished shaving a few minutes later and slipped into his tunic. "Let's go," Marcus said, reaching for his hat. "We shouldn't keep the captain waiting."

The two officers stepped outside and began walking along the edge of the quadrangle on their way to Captain Forsyth's house. On top of the stockade fence they could see one of the sentries walking slowly back and forth on the rampart, a dark silhouette against the starlit night sky.

It was getting dark earlier now, and with the setting of the sun, the temperature had already dropped by several degrees. The sentries who were on their post were wearing their overcoats, and though Marcus had not thought he would need it for the walk from his quarters to Forsyth's, he shivered in the cold night air.

"I, for one, am not looking forward to this winter," John said, giving voice to what Marcus was thinking.

"After the heat of this summer, it might be welcome," Marcus suggested. They walked down the line of married officers' quarters to Captain Forsyth's home.

Married officers' quarters were assigned by rank, with the highest-ranking officer getting the nicest quarters and the others descending in order of precedence. There were three classifications of officers' rank, with the highest being general grade, starting at brigadier general and up, then field grade, which was major, lieutenant colonel, and colonel, then company grade, which was second lieutenant, first lieutenant, and captain.

Since there were no general-grade officers in residence at Fort Reynolds, Lieutenant Colonel Pettibone, as the highest-ranking field-grade officer, had the nicest quarters; a large, two-story house with turrets and a wraparound porch. Major Conklin's house had been the commandant's quarters before the new residence was built, and it, too, was quite large and very nice. The surgeon had the next best quarters, but he would have had it regardless of his rank, for it was part of the hospital.

Other than the commander, executive officer, and surgeon, there were no field-grade officers at Fort Reynolds. That was why, when the regiment was divided into battalions, captains had to act as battalion commanders. And of all the captains, Captain Forsyth had the biggest and nicest house, by virtue of the fact that his date of rank superseded that of any other captain on the post. Even so, his quarters were little to brag about, and in any civilian town in the country, would have been considered the residence of a person of modest income.

Janet Forsyth was used to the varying degrees of comfort available to officers' wives, however, and she took it all in stride.

"When we were posted to Fort Riley we had a fine house," she said to the two young officers. "It was all brick, with a wonderful screened-in front porch, running water, and a lovely heating stove, rather than drafty old fireplaces."

"Yes, but don't forget we had also lived in a tent, Janet," Captain Forsyth said.

Janet laughed. "Heavens, how could I ever forget that?" she replied. "No, dear, all things considered, I think we are doing just fine here, and you'll have no complaints from me. And now, if you gentlemen will excuse me, I'll just get my wrap, then we can walk over to the commandant's house together."

"Did the colonel bring back any news?" Marcus asked.

"One piece of information," Forsyth answered. He took his pipe from a table next to the chair and stuck it in his pocket to have with him after dinner. Next, he filled a small leather tobacco pouch, closed it, then put it in his pocket as well. While he was doing that, he continued answering Marcus's question. "We have received orders transferring Captain Andrews to Fort Wallace, by request of the commander."

"By request of the commander?" John said in surprise. "But, Captain Forsyth, aren't we short of officers?"

Forsyth looked at Marcus with a pleased smile on his face. Marcus knew exactly why Pettibone might have lost confidence in Andrews, and yet it was obvious by John's question that Marcus had said nothing about it. It was the mark of a good officer that he didn't prattle and betray confidences.

"I will share the reason with you, Lieutenant Culpepper, because you are a young officer and I feel this will be a good object lesson for you," Forsyth said. "During the battle with Two Eagle last week, Colonel Pettibone, through Lieutenant Cavanaugh, sent a field order to Captain Andrews. Captain Andrews changed the field order."

"And that's why Pettibone wants to get rid of him? Just because he changed a field order?"

"Can you explain it to him, Cavanaugh?" Forsyth asked, as if he were the teacher, calling on one pupil to explain a problem to another pupil.

"When a field commander finds his units spread out over distances too far for normal communication, it is absolutely critical that he knows, at all times, where his distant units are, and what they are doing," Marcus explained. "Without the ability to communicate, the only way he can know this is to issue orders and be able to depend, with absolute certainty, that those orders are being carried out. When Captain Andrews changed those orders, he broke the line of communication."

"Suppose the orders are wrong?" John asked.

"As subordinate commanders in the field, we don't have the luxury of supposing that," Marcus replied.

"Very good, Lieutenant," Captain Forsyth said, beaming. "For that, you may go to the head of the class."

"Not such an honor," John teased, "when I'm the only other one in the class."

"Well, I'm all ready," Mrs. Forsyth said, coming back with her coat to rejoin the men. Both lieutenants came to attention in her presence.

"How lovely you look tonight, Mrs. Forsyth," Marcus said.

Mrs. Forsyth laughed easily, though obviously flattered by his statement. "Lieutenant, I don't hear the Irish accent in your speech that I do in so many of the men, but I do believe you've a bit of the blarney in you," she teased.

"Oh, but he's quite right, ma'am," John added quickly.

"You, too? Let's go, Edward, before they run out of nice things to say," she said to her husband.

Captain Forsyth helped her slip into her wrap, and a moment later they were walking four doors away, to the house of the post commander.

After dinner at the regimental commander's house, the Pettibones and their guests adjourned to the parlor, where Mrs. Pettibone and Mrs. Forsyth began working on a quilt while the men talked.

Colonel Pettibone lit his pipe and that was an invitation for Captain Forsyth to do the same. Within a moment their smoke filled the room with its pungent but pleasant aroma. Though neither Marcus nor John were smoking, they were drinking wine, having carried their glasses with them from the dinner table.

"I made a rather bold proposal to General Sheridan," Pettibone said. "And I must say, I do believe the general agrees with me. Of course, the decision to do what I propose must be made at the highest level—the very highest level—back in Washington. Unfortunately, I don't think anyone in that nest of politicians has the courage to make such a decision. Especially as this is an election year."

"What was your recommendation, sir?" Forsyth asked.

"Total extermination of the Indians," Pettibone answered easily.

Marcus looked up in quick surprise. "Sir, surely you don't mean exterminate?"

"Oh, I'm afraid that I do mean exterminate," Pettibone said. "That's what you do to vermin, isn't it? If we had a nest of rats in our food-storage room, wouldn't we take pains to exterminate them?"

"With all due respect, sir, these aren't rats." "In my book, Lieutenant, they are on the same order. Surely you don't regard them as our equal?"

Marcus remembered standing beside Dog Runner's body and listening to Missouri Joe tell him that though Dog Runner was an evil man who had done things that made him deserve killing, he was still a man. He had taken Missouri Joe's comment to heart, but Colonel Pettibone seemed to be disputing that basic concept.

"I regard them as men, sir. And I cannot believe you would make such a drastic proposal," Marcus said.

"I suppose I can understand your reluctance to my plan," Pettibone said. "For the truth is, when I first began thinking about it, I considered it too extreme. But the more I thought of it, the more I decided it was the right thing to do. And I give you this example. What about the Indian situation back in the States? Do you think there is any possibility of an Indian attack on New York, Boston, or Philadelphia?"

John laughed. "I don't know what Marcus thinks, but I would hardly think so," he said. "I never even saw an Indian until I came out here."

"Precisely," Pettibone said. "There is no Indian problem in the East. But two hundred years ago, when the white man first came to these shores, there were many Indians. It was not until those Indians were all killed or forced to move out that those great, civilized cities could spring forth. The way I see it, what was successful there will be successful everywhere. Any Indians we encounter should be killed or run out."

"What of the Indians who are at peace?" Marcus asked.

"Peace for an Indian, Lieutenant Cavanaugh, is merely an opportunity to plan against the whites. Eliminate the Indians, and we will enter a millennium of peace."

"Colonel Pettibone, do you honestly believe anyone will ever accept your plan?" Captain Forsyth asked.

"Yes," Pettibone said easily. "Well, not right away, and possibly not even as an official government policy. But Washington will allow it to happen. By an inference here and a closed eye there, you will see my plan eventually take shape. That is because the Indian is a terrifying creature to the people. Our people have supported a program of extermination in the past, and I've no doubt but that they will continue to support it in the future. Indians, after all, are not the same as us."

"Colonel, perhaps they are not as civilized as we, but surely you do believe that they are human beings?" Mrs. Forsyth spoke up. Most of the time the women were very quiet during such discussions, confining themselves to quilting or knitting or whatever other diversion the hostess had provided. In this case, however, Marcus could tell by the tone of her voice that Mrs. Forsyth was so opposed to and appalled by what Colonel Pettibone was saying, that she couldn't be quiet.

"No, I beg to differ with you, Mrs. Forsyth," Colonel Pettibone said. "They are not human beings, and you would know that if you had any occasion to come into contact with them." "I've seen Indians at the trading post," Mrs. Forsyth said.

"My dear, those are tame Indians," Pettibone suggested. "Consider, if you will, what it would be like if you were, for some reason, forced to live with the Indians."-

"Really, dear, is this conversation necessary?" Mrs. Pettibone asked with a shudder. "I think we have gone quite far enough."

"I suppose so," Pettibone said. He smiled. "Very well, then, on to other things. Captain Forsyth, how would you feel about a winter campaign?"

"A winter campaign?"

"Yes. I've convinced General Sheridan to let me conduct one," Pettibone went on. "Think of it . . . when the heavy snows come, where are the Indians going to be? They're going to be in their village," he said before Captain Forsyth had an opportunity to answer.

"Yes, sir, I suppose they will be," Forsyth said.

"And if, perchance, they should decide to leave, they will leave tracks through the snow so plain that the greenest recruit in the regiment will be able to follow."

"That's true. It's very difficult to lose track of them when all the ground is covered with snow," Forsyth agreed. "Do you plan to go with the first snow?"

"No. I want a good base of snow on the ground," Pettibone said. "And I want them to feel secure. I think by the second or third snowstorm they'll be perfectly content to wait out the winter. We'll track them across hill and dale, through woods and over streams, go wherever we have to, dog them until they can move no farther. Then, when they are exhausted and are inside their tents, warming themselves by the fires, the Fourth Cavalry will attack."

"I'll admit that your plan does have some merit, Colonel, but won't the Fourth be just as exhausted?" Forsyth asked.

"Oh, I'm sure we will be, Captain, I'm sure we will be," Pettibone replied. "But the difference is we will be a disciplined army. They are trained to the command and to respond to orders. The Indians, on the other hand, while fierce fighters as individuals, will not have the leadership or the discipline to go that extra step. We will lick the Indians by turning our strength against their weakness . . . our leadership against their disorder. I have never forgotten one of the first axioms I learned at West Point. It was by Euripides." He turned to Marcus. "You are a recent graduate, Mr. Cavanaugh. Do you remember it?"

"Yes, sir," Marcus said. "'Ten men, wisely led, are worth a hundred without a head.'" Colonel Pettibone beamed proudly and shook his head in the affirmative.

"Good man, Lieutenant, good man. Soon, I hope you shall have the opportunity to see that axiom put to the test."

It was already past taps when Marcus took his nightly walk around the post that night. It was cold enough for him to wear his overcoat, and he had his hands stuck down into the pockets as he strolled across the parade grounds. The flagpole, empty now, was a slender finger pointing toward a sky that was filled with thousands of brilliant points of light. On a night this clear Marcus could even see a fine dust of blue behind the stars.

"Post number eight! Eleven o'clock, and all is well!"

The call was from the farthest corner of the fort, a distant, barely heard voice.

"Post number seven! Eleven o'clock, and all is well!"

This call was closer and easier to hear.

"Post number six! Eleven o'clock, and all is well!"

This call was so close that it made Marcus jump, and he looked around to see the sentry of post number six very close by.

The call continued on until it reached the guard house. It reminded Marcus of a train whistle, quiet in the distance when one first hears it, gradually getting louder until it was right upon you, then growing quieter again.

"Good evenin', Lieutenant Cavanaugh," the sentry at post number six said as Marcus passed him by. The sentry saluted and Marcus returned his salute.

On the far side of the parade ground, just outside

the stables, Marcus saw a small fire burning. He knew that it was Missouri Joe, for, although the scout and his Indian wife had been offered a place to stay, they preferred pitching their own tent out on the fort grounds. He started toward it, and as he knew he would be, was greeted by Missouri Joe before he got any closer than thirty yards.

"So tell me, boy, how was the food at the colonel's house?" Missouri Joe called from the dark.

"Where are you?" Marcus asked. "I can't see you."

Marcus heard Missouri Joe chuckle. "That's 'cause you ain't learned the Indian trick of seein' in the dark."

Marcus followed the voice until he finally saw Missouri Joe's shadow. When he got closer, he was able to recognize the man.

"What do you mean, 'Indian trick'?" Marcus asked. "There's no trick to it. Either you can see in the dark, or you can't."

"That's where you're wrong, boy," Missouri Joe said. "Look, I'll show you. Look over in the corner of the stable pen there. What do you see?"

"Two horses," Marcus said. "No, wait. There's only one. Or . . . maybe there aren't any at all. It might just be shadow."

Missouri Joe chuckled. "You was right the first time," he said. "There are two horses there." He pointed to his eyes. "See, the Indians has figured out that the middle part of your eye is what you see with in the daytime. But at nighttime you see with the outside part of your eye. Iffen you try to look right at somethin', you're tryin' to look with your daytime eyes and it'll go away. Now, look over there again, only don't look right at the corner of the stable. Look just to one side."

Marcus did as he was instructed, and to his amazement, he saw that there were two horses standing there. Then, to test the theory, he looked right at them, and they disappeared. "I'll be damned!"

Now it was Missouri Joe's time to chuckle. "Thought you might like that," he said. "I don't show that to just ever'body. Sometimes a fella likes to keep just a little advantage to hisself."

"Why did you show me?"

"I don't know," Missouri Joe admitted. "You seem like a bright enough fella to pick it up. Want some coffee?"

"Yes," Marcus said, thinking it might help warm him.

Missouri Joe said something in a guttural language, and a large shadow loomed up from the ground behind him, then moved to the fire. It was Moon Cow Woman, though Marcus had not noticed her before. She poured a cup of coffee, then brought it to him, smiling broadly and saying something as she handed it to him.

"Thanks," Marcus said.

Missouri Joe chuckled again. "She said you was the prettiest man she'd ever seen, an' she would sure like to have you share the buffalo robes with her sometime."

Marcus had just started to take a swallow of his coffee, and he coughed in surprise, spraying some of it out. He felt his cheeks flame in embarrassment.

Missouri Joe said something to Moon Cow Woman and she laughed, then sat back down.

"You don't have to worry none about her, boy. She ain't gonna rape you or nothin'." "She is a very, uh, frank person," Marcus said.

"What's that mean?"

"It means she says just what she thinks, without holding anything back."

"Yeah, she does do that," Missouri Joe said. "But then, I reckon most Indians is like that. That's what makes it so hard for them an' whites to deal with each other. Most whites talk all aroun' a subject, sayin' ever'thin' but what they really mean. Most Indians, on the other hand, say exactly what they mean. You can see how somethin' like that can cause lots of confusion."

"To listen to you, Joe, one would think that the Indians are always right and we are always wrong. But if you are trying to convince me, you are talking to the wrong person. You forget, I have already seen examples of their atrocities ... at the stagecoach way station and at the wagon of the innocent settlers they killed."

"No, sir, I ain't takin' up for 'em, don't get me wrong on that point. Once the Indian gets to fightin', there ain't no more savage fighter in nature. He's like a rattlesnake, he has no conscience. A rattlesnake can strike and kill a four-year-old little girl or a grown man, an' it don't make no difference to him. A Indian ain't no different from a rattlesnake. He can do the same thing."

Marcus took a drink of his coffee before he replied. "Well, in that, at least, you and Colonel Pettibone concur. The colonel thinks the Indians are the same as wild animals."

"Iffen you want to know the funny thing about that," Joe said, "most Indians would agree with him. In fact, they'd consider it a compliment. You see, Indians set a great store about them being just one of the parts of what the Great Spirit has created. They don't set themselves above animals, no how."

"Missouri Joe, if you have such an affinity for the Indians, how can you work for the Army? How can you scout against the Indians?"

"Same reason a lot of Indians work for the Army. Long as there's Indians like Two Eagles, hungry to make war against the whites instead of learning to live with 'em, there's gonna be men like Colonel Pettibone who thinks the only good Indian is a dead Indian. If there weren't any whites like Pettibone, Two Eagles couldn't get anyone to follow him. And it's a cinch Two Eagles can't make war against the whites all by hisself."

"What do you mean, Two Eagles couldn't get anyone to follow him? He's a chief, isn't he? His people don't have any choice."

"Boy, you got a heap to learn about Indians," Missouri Joe said. "If a Indian can get someone to follow him, he's a chief. If he can't, he ain't. It's as simple as that."

When Marcus returned to his quarters, he read the letter from Sally. As she had suggested, she was using him for a diary, and she told him all about her daily life, including a young man on an adjoining plantation that her father wanted her to marry.

After finishing the letter, Marcus took out a sheet of writing paper, his gold-tip pen, and began writing. He made sure to tell Sally about his recent experiences in battle, the upcoming winter campaign, and the Indian trick Missouri Joe taught him. Admitting he had little experience in the matters of marriage, he advised her to seek out those who did.

After he'd finished, he blotted the paper, folded it, sealed it in an envelope, and placed it on his hat. Tomorrow he would take it to the orderly room and drop it in the mail slot.

8

When the regiment turned out for reveille the next morning, Missouri Joe's tent was gone. There was no trace of him or his wife, and none of the sentries could recall when they left. Since he had two horses and a loaded travois, he couldn't have left without going through the gate, but the gate guards swore they saw nothing.

It was more than just a mystery to Colonel Pettibone. To him it was a serious matter, and he called all the officers together in the officers' side of the sutler's store.

"Last night, sometime between sundown and sunup, the scout known as Missouri Joe left this fort," Pettibone told them. "I am concerned about this for the following reasons. Number one." Pettibone held up his finger and fixed every officer in the room with his steely glare. "The fact that he was able to exit this post without being detected tells me that anyone who wishes could enter Fort Reynolds in the same way. Gentlemen, with our guards this lax, we might well wake up one morning and find this fort occupied by the Indians."

There were a few mumbles of concern and guilt among the officers, particularly the lower-ranking officers who shared the duty of officer of the day.

Colonel Pettibone held up two fingers. "The second reason I am concerned is that yesterday I brought back from Fort Wallace permission to conduct a winter campaign against the Indians. I am afraid that Missouri Joe may have gone to warn Two Eagles of my intentions."

Now there was a mumbling of surprise. None of the veterans had ever conducted a winter campaign against the Indians, nor had they ever heard of one. The Indians were generally dormant in the winter, and the Cavalry usually stayed inside the post, their biggest worry being the collection of wood for the fires.

"Colonel Pettibone, excuse me, sir," Marcus said. "Missouri Joe wouldn't jeopardize the safety of this fort."

"The man's an Indian lover, Mr. Cavanaugh."

"Because we were talking last night. He is as anxious to get rid of Two Eagles as we are. He thinks that all the Indians are being made to suffer because of what Two Eagles is doing." "You were talking with Missouri Joe last night?"

"Yes, sir."

"What time?"

"It was a little after eleven, sir. I remember, because I heard the guards' call."

"I see," Pettibone said. He stroked his beard for a moment as he looked out over the assembled officers. "Gentlemen," he finally said. "I want every man who pulled guard duty last night to be given one week of extra duty as punishment for allowing Missouri Joe to leave the post unobserved. I want the officer who was officer of the day, the sergeant of the guard, and the corporals of the guard to remain on guard duty for one week without relief. And, beginning tonight, we will double the number of men on guard detail. This fort must be made secure. Do I make myself clear?"

"Yes, sir!" all the officers answered as one. "Very well, you are dismissed. Captain Forsyth, I would like for you and Mr. Cavanaugh to remain behind."

Marcus watched the other officers file out, and he caught the look of concern in John's face as his friend glanced back toward him. The expression in Pettibone's voice indicated that he hadn't asked them to remain behind for a pleasant visit. Marcus felt like a schoolboy who had been summoned before the principal.

Pettibone walked over to the door and stood staring out for a long moment as if making certain that all the officers were beyond earshot. Marcus and Captain Forsyth remained behind. Marcus looked over at his fellow officer, and Forsyth raised his finger to his lips, signaling him to be quiet.

Finally, with a sigh, Pettibone turned away from the

door. He was carrying his riding quirt and tapped it against his right thigh.

"Captain Forsyth, have you no more control over your officers than to allow a young second lieutenant to breach security in such a way?"

"Sir, I protest," Marcus started, but Pettibone held out his hand in a demand that Marcus hold his tongue.

"I am not speaking to you, Lieutenant. I am speaking to your commander. When an officer makes a mistake it affects not only himself, but others as well. In this case your mistake has cost Captain Forsyth dearly. I want you to know that Captain Forsyth's inability to command, as evidenced by your action, will reflect unfavorably upon his next fitness report."

"But, sir," Marcus said. "With all due respect, it wasn't Captain Forsyth who spoke with Missouri Joe. It was me!"

Pettibone turned toward him, his eyes flashing in anger. "I am the commanding officer of this regiment. It is my duty to see to it that my subordinate officers exercise control over their subordinates."

"But I didn't say anything to him that would in any way be a breach of security." "Lieutenant!" Pettibone said sharply. "Marcus, for God's sake, be quiet," Forsyth pleaded.

"Yes, sir," Marcus said, his face burning in anger and embarrassment. He was absolutely innocent of any wrongdoing, yet he was not only in trouble, he had managed, somehow, to get his commander in trouble as well. And in these days of long, slow promotions, a bad fitness report could condemn a man to stagnate in rank for years. It was quite possible that he had just ruined Forsyth's career, and he was devastated by that thought.

"I will leave it up to you, Captain, the means you choose to discipline Lieutenant Cavanaugh. I might suggest, however, that a two-week suspension of duty would be in order. I trust Lieutenant Culpepper can fill in in Cavanaugh's absence?"

"Yes, sir," Forsyth said.

"What about you, Lieutenant? Have you any reason to believe Lieutenant Culpepper could not serve in your stead? You have been responsible for some of his training, I believe?"

"Yes, sir, I have been. And there is no reason at all why Lieutenant Culpepper cannot take over my duties. He is an excellent officer, sir."

"And one who knows when to keep his mouth shut," Colonel Pettibone said. "Very well, gentlemen, you are dismissed."

Marcus and Forsyth saluted Pettibone. The colonel returned it, then quickly walked out of the room, leaving the two chastised officers alone.

"I'm sorry, Captain," Marcus said. "But I swear to you, I said nothing to Missouri Joe last night that would give him cause to leave the post. And I certainly gave him no military information."

"I believe you, Marcus," Forsyth said. He sighed, then smiled wanly. "But when we accepted our commissions, we weren't guaranteed fair treatment for our entire careers. Things like this happen."

"Captain, what exactly does a two-week suspension mean?"

"Just what it says," Forsyth answered. "For two weeks you won't be allowed to perform any of your regular duties."

"How about irregular duties?" Marcus asked. "What do you mean?"

"I mean I would like to go find Missouri Joe and bring him back."

Forsyth scratched his head for a moment as he studied Marcus.

"That could be dangerous," he warned. "I'm aware of that, sir. But it will be worth the danger if it will relieve Colonel Pettibone of his suspicions. And it might get you and me out of hot water."

"If it doesn't work, and the colonel finds out about it, it could get us in even deeper," Forsyth said. "And if I let you go, I don't know how to keep him from finding out."

"I have an idea of how I might do it. As you recall, I reported for duty directly from the academy. I still have thirty days' graduation leave coming. Is there anything that says I can't take fifteen days of leave during my suspension of duty?"

Captain Forsyth smiled. "Nothing that I know of," he said. "Put in for the leave, and I'll sign the papers. But, Marcus," he added. "Yes, sir?"

"If you are serious about doing this . . . about going

out to look for Missouri Joe, don't go in uniform. A single hunter, prospector, or traveler can sometimes move around without raising too much fuss. But a soldier in uniform is just asking for trouble." "I'll be the most unmilitary person you ever saw," Marcus said.

Captain Forsyth smiled broadly. "That's going to be hard for you to do. You've been in the Army less than a year, but I already have the feeling that if you were cut, you would bleed army blue."

Marcus pulled his parka about him more tightly and, standing in the stirrups of his saddle, looked down on the other side of the hill his horse had just climbed. He had been out for eight days, and last night was the first storm of winter. It was a very heavy snow and the world before him was harsh white and stark black, covered with the newly fallen snow. About a mile and a half away he saw a small encampment, consisting of two tepees and a campfire.

Marcus did not happen upon the encampment by accident. He had smelled the woodsmoke when he awoke earlier this morning, and he merely followed his nose to this point.

"Well, horse, I do believe that is them," Marcus said. "One of the tepees, anyway, looks like the one Missouri Joe had pitched inside the fort."

Marcus had accustomed himself to the complete isolation of the wide-open spaces by talking to his horse, just to hear the sound of a human voice . . . even his own. He leaned over and patted his horse on the neck.

"I hope Missouri Joe is as friendly to me out here as he was inside."

Marcus started riding toward the little camp. He could see a woman working around the fire, and from the size of her, knew that it was Moon Cow Woman. A moment later he saw Missouri Joe, then, to his surprise, another woman. There hadn't been a second woman with them when they were in camp.

He knew they had seen him by now, for his approach was as visible as black ink on white paper. His horse left a trail in the snow behind him; a long, dark scar on the face of the white hill. The second woman went back into one of the tepees and didn't come back out.

"Hello, the camp," he called when he was within hailing distance.

"Lieutenant Cavanaugh? Do that be you?" Missouri Joe called back.

"Yes, it's me," Marcus replied.

"What are you doin' out here?" Missouri Joe asked. "And why is it you ain't in your soldier suit? You ain't left the Army, have you?" "No," Marcus said. He swung down from the horse and handed over a packet of coffee beans. "I'll trade you some of this for some you already made," he offered.

"Sure," Missouri Joe said. "Moon Cow Woman, pour the boy a cup of coffee."

"Pretty man like coffee Moon Cow Woman," she said, smiling broadly. That was the first time Marcus had ever heard her speak in anything except her own guttural tongue.

"I didn't know she could speak English," he said.

"It's just a trick Indians use sometimes," Missouri Joe said. "If the soldiers don't know she can speak our lingo, they sometimes say things that's helpful."

"Like what?" Marcus asked sharply. Could it be that the colonel was right? Had they overheard some information, and were they taking it to Two Eagles?

"Don't get your dander up," Missouri Joe said, laughing. "It ain't like we're listenin' for a chance to do any spyin' or anythin'. What are you doin' out here, anyway?"

"I've come to take you back with me." "Take me back? Look here, boy, you plan-nin' on arrestin' me for somethin'? 'Cause if you are, I wouldn't take too kindly to that. Most 'specially since I ain't done nothin' wrong."

"No, nothing like that," Marcus said. "I want to take you back to save my career. And Captain Forsyth's." Marcus went on to explain Pettibone's reaction when he learned that Missouri Joe had left.

Missouri Joe listened to it all, then he laughed. "Boy, iffen you ask me, you'd be better off gettin' plumb on out of the Army. Any outfit that would let a crazy man like Pettibone be its head man ain't worth hangin' around."

"I have no intention of leaving the Army," Marcus said.

"I see. And what if I tell you I don't want to go back? What will you do, then?"

"I'll take you back."

"How?"

"I'm not exactly sure yet," Marcus said. "But I'll find a way."

Missouri Joe laughed again. "You know, son, I believe you would at that," he said. "All right, I'll go back with you. Fact is, I'll do better'n that. I'll give you somethin' to take back with you."

"What's that?" Marcus asked.

"Two Eagles has gathered all his warriors together into one big village. They're callin' it Oushata. Sasha told us about it, and where it is."

"That's Moon Cow Woman's little sister. She's the one you seen when you was ridin' into camp. She was married to Dog Runner. She slipped into the Fort last night. We figured Pettibone wouldn't take to her none too kind, 'specially since she'd been livin' with Two Eagles's band. So we figured the best thing to do would be to get her to some place safe. That's why we left. We was plannin' on comin' back, once we got Sasha settled."

"And this Sasha . . . Dog Runner's widow . . . knows where Two Eagles's camp is?"

"Yep." Missouri Joe stared at Cavanaugh for a minute.

"Can you get me into it?"

"I knew that was coming," Missouri Joe said, shaking his head. "That's a fool notion, son." "I need to see it, Joe."

"You don't have to see it, boy. I can tell you exactly where it is."

"The colonel will not believe me unless I observe it with my own eyes."

Missouri Joe spit and stroked his beard. "Boy, you're askin' a hell of a lot," he said.

"I know," Marcus replied.

"Pretty man know Two Eagles want kill him?" Moon Cow Woman asked.

"Yes," Marcus said. "I know.

"Pretty man very brave," Moon Cow Woman said. "My man take you."

"Wait a minute, now. Just hold on there, Moon Cow Woman," Missouri Joe said.

"You take him," Moon Cow Woman said again, and her voice was so resolute that even Marcus could tell that she didn't plan to argue about it.

"All right, all right, I'll take him. But if we get caught and I get hung out over some fire, I don't expect to see you throwin' any wood into the flames."

"I will cry much," Moon Cow Woman said.

"Oh, yeah, that will make me feel real good," Missouri Joe teased, and Marcus smiled because he knew the issue was settled now, and he would be able to count on Missouri Joe.

Sasha came out of the other tepee then. She was thin and young, with large, doelike eyes and clear, olive skin. She looked at Marcus with undisguised curiosity. He was surprised because even beneath all the winter clothes she was wearing, he could see that she was a very pretty woman. Sasha said something in her own language but it didn't seem to have the same, guttural quality it had when Moon Cow Woman spoke it. Instead it had a lilting, almost musical quality.

"She wants to know if you are the one who killed her man," Missouri Joe said. Missouri Joe looked at the pretty young Indian woman and even to Marcus's untrained ear, he knew that he was telling her yes. She just continued to stare at him.

"Missouri Joe, you told me Dog Runner was your wife's cousin. You didn't tell me her sister was married to him."

"Well, he was her cousin," Missouri Joe said. "But Indians ain't that particular about it. You don't get no brothers marryin' sisters or nothin' like that. But cousins is fair game. And I didn't tell you he was married to my wife's sister 'cause I figured you done felt bad enough already 'bout killin' him."

"Yeah, I guess I did."

Sasha said something again, and again her voice had a lilting, musical quality to it . . . like the sound of wind bells.

"What did she say?"

"She thanked you for killing Dog Runner and setting her free."

"What am I supposed to say?" Marcus asked. "I can hardly say 'you're welcome' to something like that."

Sasha spoke again, except this time, before Marcus could even ask what she had said, Moon Cow Woman spoke out harshly to the young woman. The two exchanged brief, angry words while Missouri Joe laughed. Sasha turned to go back into her tepee.

"What is it?" Marcus asked. "What was that all about?"

"Sasha offered to sleep with you tonight," Missouri Joe said. "She said she has no man and you have no woman. It is cold, and you could keep each other warm."

"Oh, no, I'd . ."

Missouri Joe laughed again and held up his hand. "Don't worry none about it," he said, interrupting Marcus's protestations. "Moon Cow Woman done took care of it for you. She said you was her pretty man and if you didn't share her robes, you sure as hell wasn't going to share the robes with Sasha."

"Missouri Joe, doesn't this kind of talk bother, you?" Marcus asked.

"Why?" Missouri Joe replied. "You mean am I jealous 'cause Moon Cow Woman wants to roll around in the furs with you?"

"Well, yes."

"Why the hell should I be?" Missouri Joe asked. "Look at her. You ever seen anyone that ugly?"

"Well, I . . ."

"Come on, tell me the truth now. You ever seen anyone any uglier than Moon Cow Woman?"

"I admit that she's not what I would call a very pretty woman," Marcus said as diplomatically as possible.

"No, she ain't. She's ugly as a wart hog. So, do you think I really believe you'd ever sleep with her?"

"Not willingly," Marcus agreed.

"Hell, no; not you nor anybody else I ever met. And iffen someone was to come along who actually would sleep with her, you don't reckon he'd really try and take her away from me, do you?"

"I wouldn't think so," Marcus said.

"Well, then, that's it, Lieutenant. Moon Cow Woman can have all the cravin' she wants. She can see pretty men day in and day out as far as I'm concerned. I got me no worries. Ain't nobody wants Moon Cow Woman but me." "Missouri Joe, you are a most unusual man," Marcus said.

"Ain't I, though? Now, what say we get inside out of the cold, while the women fix us up somethin' to eat? Iffen we're gonna sneak into Oushata tonight, we got some plans need to be made."

9

"Here," Missouri Joe said, handing a buffalo robe to Marcus. "This'll keep you warmer than anything you got to wear, and besides that, it won't stand out like that white man's coat you got on."

Marcus wrapped himself in the robe, then smiled at Missouri Joe. The scout was right, it was warmer.

"Iffen the soldiers had any sense they'd throw away them cloth coats the Army gives 'em an' make coats out of buffalo hide," Missouri Joe went on.

"Maybe I'll write a letter suggesting that the Army adopt buffalo coats," Marcus said.

Missouri Joe grunted. "Yeah, well, that all depends on whether you live through this little adventure we're takin' tonight," he said. "Now, when we get started, you follow me, you do ever'thin' I tell you to do, an' you don't say nothin'."

"Don't worry, I will. All I want to do is see that village for myself."

"Yeah, well I'd like to see it from outside. I don't particular want to stand tied up to a pole in the inner circle, lookin' out on the village through a bonfire, if you know what I mean." "Yes, I think I know what you mean," Marcus said. Moon Cow Woman came up to Marcus then, and to his surprise began sniffing around on him like a dog. "What is she doing?"

"Pretty man smell too pretty," Moon Cow Woman said.

"What?" Missouri Joe said. He walked over to Marcus and took a couple of whiffs himself. "Damn me if she ain't right," he said. "Boy, you smell like soap an' shavin' cream an' hair tonic. We got to do somethin' about that." "What do you have in mind?"

"Moon Cow Woman, take care of him," Missouri Joe said.

Moon Cow Woman said something in her own language, and Missouri Joe interpreted. "Take offen your shirt," he said. "Iffen you got long-handles on underneath, strip it off, too, so's you're down to the bare skin."

"What are you going to do?" Marcus asked as he did what Missouri Joe told him.

"We're gonna cover your body with burned wood ash," Missouri Joe said. "That'll make you smell like smoke. You see, bein' as smoke's a natural scent, it don't spook Indians or animals. It'll cover you up real good."

Moon Cow Woman and Sasha rubbed Marcus's body down with ash, then added some grease of their own.

"Little buffalo grease will help," Missouri Joe explained. Missouri Joe took a bottle of whiskey from one of his packs, pulled the cork, then took several long swallows before he recorked it and returned the bottle without offering a drink to Marcus.

When she finished with him, Moon Cow Woman smiled at Marcus. "Now, pretty man no smell pretty," she said.

Missouri Joe took another whiff, then turned his head. "Whew," he said. "Even *I* think you stink."

"They may never let me back onto the fort," Marcus said, grimacing.

"Well, come on, let's go. If we get to movin' now, we can be to the village after dark." Marcus mounted his horse, and he and Missouri Joe rode away from the little camp. Though the snow wasn't deep enough to cause the horses a great deal of difficulty, it was enough to cause them to be very deliberate with their footing, so the going was a little slower than normal. They plodded on across the cold terrain for the rest of the day, stopping only a few times to give the horses a rest.

Finally, just after dark, Missouri Joe stopped and swung down.

"Leave the horses here," he said.

"Are we near the camp?"

"No more'n mile off in that direction," Missouri Joe said, pointing to the north. "We'll walk on down and take a look."

"What's the best approach to avoid their guards?" Marcus asked.

Missouri Joe grunted. "Guards? Boy, Indians don't have guards."

"What do you mean? They have to have guards. Their villages would be wide open, otherwise."

"They are."

"But this is supposed to be a war camp."

"It is. But there won't be no guards. Look, do your soldier boys like to stand guard in the middle of the night when its cold, when they're tired, or when somethin' else is goin' on?"

"Well, no, I wouldn't say they like it." "Then why do they do it?"

"Because they are ordered to."

"Well, there you go," Missouri Joe said. "You can order a soldier to do somethin' and he will. But no Indian can order another Indian to do anythin'. An Indian does only what he wants to do, and none of 'em want to stand guard."

"That's amazing," Marcus said.

"Don't matter. Like as not half the camp will be up dancin' and singin', anyway. This bein' a war camp composed of Indians from different villages, I reckon they'll be goin' way into the night, sharin' tales of great deeds and the like. That means that even if they don't have guards, they'll be plenty of people awake, so we'll have to be careful."

The village of Oushata was pitched on the banks of a small stream. Though the sky was heavily overcast and threatening more snow, the snow that had already fallen managed to hold what light there was so they could see better than under normal night conditions. Marcus didn't even have to use his newly learned night-vision technique to see nearly two hundred tepees. It helped that in the exact center of the village was a large fire with several Indians dancing around it.

"No doubt about it," Missouri Joe said. "They're gettin' themselves worked up for somethin' pretty big."

"Do you think we could get in close enough to find out what is going on?" Marcus asked.

"Boy, you ain't got much sense, but I'll give it to you for guts," Missouri Joe said. "Come on, let's see what we can do."

They walked for a mile over the hard ground, the only sounds being the crunching of snow under their feet and their breath, which blew out like little steam clouds and drifted away. When they reached the south end of the village, several dogs came bounding toward them. Missouri Joe reached down into his satchel and took out a handful of bones. He scattered them on the snow, and the dogs went to the food.

"Reach down and touch a couple of them," Missouri Joe said. "That way the other dogs will smell them on you and won't think you're a stranger."

Marcus reached down, intending to pet one of the dogs, but the dog snapped at him. Then he saw Missouri Joe push one of the dogs' heads down in the snow and run his hands up and down the dog's back. When he let go, the dog was glad enough to get away. Marcus did the same thing, then the two men were able to walk through the pack without difficulty.

Marcus could hear the rhythmic thump of the drums, the high-pitched tweet of an eagle- bone whistle, and the monotone chants of the songs. He could see the golden wash of light on the sides of the lodge, but from here he could see none of the actual dancers.

The two men suddenly heard women's voices and Missouri Joe held up his hand, signaling a stop. When Missouri Joe dropped down to one knee, Marcus did the same thing, and they moved close to the side of one of the tepees. Three women walked by just in front of them, so involved in their own conversation that they paid no attention to what was going on around them.

When the women were gone, they moved a little closer. They finally made it to the center circle, where a large bubble of golden light from the big bonfire lit the faces of the young warriors who were dancing. In the shadows around the outside of the fire light, the very young and the very old, who were not permitted to take part in the dance because of their ages, sat in twos and threes, quietly watching. Missouri Joe pulled the robe over the top of his head, then sat on a fallen log, and Marcus sat beside him.

The music stopped and one of the dancers moved to the center of the circle. He stood facing the fire for a moment, then raised both his hands over his head. His robe slid down and Marcus saw that he was barechested, except for a necklace of bear's teeth. One half of his face was painted red, the other half yellow.

"That there is Two Eagles," Missouri Joe said quietly.

It began snowing again, but the snow didn't stop Two Eagles. He stood like a statue under the great white flakes and continued to stare into the fire. Finally he turned away from the fire and began speaking. Marcus couldn't understand what he was saying, but he could tell from the reaction of those listening to him that Two Eagles was a powerful speaker, a man who could move his listeners.

"Know anything about the town of Willow Springs?" Missouri Joe asked.

"Yes. That's the next terminus of the railroad," Marcus said.

"How many folks live there?"

"Two or three hundred, I would guess," Marcus said. "And it's growing every day." "Yeah, well, it ain't gonna grow much more. Two Eagles is plannin' on attackin' it." "When?"

"A couple of days yet," Missouri Joe said. "They're waitin' on a few more to join them. 'Course, if this snow keeps on, that might hold 'em back, too."

"We've got to get back to the fort," Marcus said. "Colonel Pettibone must be told of this." "That mean you've seen enough?"

"Yes."

"I'm glad of that," Missouri Joe said. "The way you are, I wasn't sure but what you'd want me to go up an' talk to the fella. Come on, let's get out of here."

The two men retraced their steps back through the camp. The snow was falling even heavier now, though it had not yet covered their footprints. Unfortunately, someone else had also noticed their footprints, and when Marcus and Missouri Joe reached the edge of the village, they saw two Indians standing there, looking at the filling, but still-deep scar which led down from the nearby woods. It was obvious to the Indians that someone had just come into the camp, and they looked as if they were on the verge of sounding an alarm.

"Oh, oh," Missouri Joe said. "We'd better take care of these two before they have the whole camp down on us."

Missouri Joe said something in a low, guttural voice, and the two Indians turned around toward them.

"Get your knife out, boy. You're gonna need it," Missouri Joe hissed. Missouri Joe dropped his robe to give him freedom of movement, and Marcus did the same.

Marcus had never been in a knife fight in his life. He pulled his knife, then looked over at Missouri Joe and assumed a stance similar to the scout's. He was crouched a little, right arm out, blade projecting from across the upturned palm between the thumb and index finger, with the point moving back and forth.

The Indian lunged but Marcus dodged him easily. Then Marcus realized that the techniques he had learned in fencing could be applied here; precision, speed, timing, and distance. The fencing attack coordinated hand and footwork with a minimum of wasted motion. Success depended on split-second timing; fractions of an inch in distance; and sound, tactical judgment.

Foiled on his first attempt, the Indian danced in for a second, raising his left hand toward Marcus's face to mask his action. He feinted with his right, the knife hand, outside Marcus's left arm as if he were going to go in over it. In the same movement, when Marcus automatically reacted against it, the Indian brought his knife hand back down so fast it was a blur, and caught Marcus under his arm.

The knife went through Cavanaugh's heavy clothing, but the layers of cloth protected him from any serious wound. Even so, he could feel the knife searing like a branding iron along his ribs, opening a long gash in the tight ridges of muscle. He could also feel the blood down his side, and for the moment, he had no idea how badly he might be hurt.

Marcus brought his left hand down sharply and knocked away the Indian's knife. He jabbed quickly with his right hand, sending the blade of his knife into the Indian's diaphragm, just under the ribs.

They stood that way for a few moments, Marcus twisting the blade in the wound, trying to make certain his stab was fatal and struggling to stay on his feet in spite of the pain burning in his side.

Finally the Indian began to collapse, expelling a long, life-surrendering sigh as he did. As Marcus felt him going he turned the knife, blade edge up, letting the Indian's body tear itself off by its own weight. It cut deeply along the ribs, disemboweling him. When the Indian hit the ground, he flapped once or twice, then lay still while blood and the contents of his opened stomach stained the white, then was covered by the new snow.

Marcus looked over to see Missouri Joe finishing off his own opponent.

"You all right?" Marcus asked.

"Yeah, how about you?"

"I'm fine. Let's get out of here."

It wasn't until later, when they had made it back to their horses and Missouri Joe saw Marcus wincing with pain while he was getting mounted, that he realized Marcus was hurt.

"Let me take a look at it."

Missouri Joe opened Marcus's shirt, then chuckled.

"You was some lucky," he said. "The cut don't go deep at all." He started scooping up snow.

"What are you doing?"

"I'm gonna pack snow in between your shirt and the wound. It'll stop the bleedin' and ease the pain."

At first the snow was so cold that Marcus could barely stand it, but after a few minutes a numbing warmth began to spread around his side. And, as Missouri Joe promised, it completely killed the pain. The two men rode off into the snowstorm, swallowed up by the swirling flakes of white before they went more than fifty yards.

It was just after dark the next evening when the guard at the front gate of Fort Reynolds challenged Marcus and Missouri Joe. Marcus saw that in addition to the guard on the ground, there was another on the parapet. That meant that Colonel Pettibone's order to double the sentries was still in effect.

"Who goes there?" the guard on the ground challenged.

"A friend," Marcus responded. "I'm Lieutenant Cavanaugh, this is Missouri Joe, a scout for the United States Cavalry."

"Advance, friend, and be recognized," the guard said, continuing the formula for challenge.

Marcus and Missouri Joe rode on up to the gate, where a small lantern was burning. The soldier turned the lantern to cast a light and he looked at them closely, then came to attention.

"Christ, Lieutenant Cavanaugh, it is you! You look awful, sir!"

"I must see Captain Forsyth and Colonel Pettibone at once," Marcus said.

The guard pointed across the quadrangle to the brightly lit sutler's store.

"You'll find 'em in there. Fact is, you'll find ever'one in there. Case you forgot, sir, this here is Thanksgivin' an' the regiment is havin' a Thanksgivin' party for all the officers and the men. That is, 'ceptin' those of us on guard."

"Don't let it bother you any, soldier," Marcus said. "I don't think they'll be there much longer."

Marcus and Missouri Joe rode across the quadrangle, then tied their horses at the hitching rail in front of the sutler's store. Someone was singing inside, and Marcus recognized the high,-clear voice of Sergeant

Patrick O'Daigh, the best tenor in the regiment. Like many singers and musicians, Sergeant O'Daigh had used his talent to get his stripes, for such men were good for troop morale, and commanders would go to any length to keep them. O'Daigh was singing "The Dew Is on the Grass Lorena." No one was dancing at this precise moment, for this was the entertainment part of the program.

"Boy, when we go inside there, you reckon I could slip over an' get me a little drink of whiskey without bein' noticed?"

Marcus laughed. "Believe me, there is no way we're going to go in there without being noticed," he said.

When they stepped up onto the porch, Marcus glanced through the window, where he saw the bunting and party decorations, the bright dresses, and the clean, blue uniforms. With his ten-day growth of beard, his dirty clothes, and rancid smell, he was going to make quite an intrusion on this party. He took a deep breath, then pushed in through the door.

One of the laundresses, not recognizing either of the men, screamed. Lieutenant Humes, who did recognize Marcus, spoke aloud what everyone was thinking.

"My God, Cavanaugh, you are disgusting!" Colonel Pettibone turned and bellowed out loudly, "Lieutenant Cavanaugh, what is the meaning of this?"

"Colonel Pettibone, Captain Forsyth, I must speak with you at once."

"You go over to the headquarters room, mister,"

Pettibone said. "I'll deal with you when this dance is over."

"Sir, this is an emergency!" Marcus said. "Captain Forsyth?" Marcus added, pleading his case with his next higher commander.

"Colonel, if you will not receive this officer now, I shall write a report to General Sheridan registering my protest," Forsyth said.

Pettibone looked at Captain Forsyth, who, in his full-dress uniform, cut quite a formidable figure, then contrasted him with Marcus, who looked like a destitute trail bum.

"Very well, Captain Forsyth," Pettibone agreed. "But it had better be important or it is I who will be wrinng the letter to the general." Pettibone looked back over the curious faces of those at the party, then toward the bandstand. "Bandmaster, if you would please, continue the music."

The bandmaster turned to his musicians, tapped his baton a couple of times, then started a song. The music was "Put Your Little Foot," but Marcus couldn't help but wonder if he had just stuck his big foot right into it.

The officer of the day looked up in surprise when he saw the four men come into the regimental headquarters building . . . two in full-dress uniform, and two barely recognizable as civilized men. The officer of the day stood as Colonel Pettibone swept by his desk, leading his little entourage into his office. Once inside the office, Pettibone, his eyes still blazing in anger, turned toward Marcus.

"Mister, how dare you present yourself before the officers, ladies, and men of the Fourth Cavalry Regiment in such a . . . a . . . disgraceful condition!" he said. "What is so important that you could interrupt a regimental celebration?"

"They are related, Colonel," Marcus said. "I am dressed like this because last night Missouri Joe and I sneaked into Two Eagles's new war camp. We listened to Two Eagles and his bunch plan an attack on Willow Springs tomorrow."

Marcus studied Pettibone's face. This was it . . . the moment of truth. Was Colonel Pettibone a petty tyrant, or was he a good officer? If he was a petty tyrant, he would continue raving at Marcus. If he was a good officer, he would turn his concern to the news Marcus brought him.

"How long would it take this command to reach the village?" he asked.

"We were slowed quite a bit by the snowstorm this morning," Marcus said. "Although it was a blessing, because we killed a couple of their warriors, and the storm that slowed us kept the Indians from finding us. I think if we left within the hour we could be there sometime tomorrow morning."

"If we leave within thirty minutes and push it hard, can we reach the village before dawn?" "Yes, sir," Marcus said. "I believe we can." Pettibone stepped out of his office and spoke to the officer of the day.

"Lieutenant, send your runner for the trumpeter."

"Yes, sir."

When the trumpeter came in a few moments later, Pettibone asked that he blow officers' call. The effect of the call was immediate, because they could hear the music stop from the sutler's store.

"Lieutenant Cavanaugh," Colonel Pettibone said as they were waiting for the officers to assemble, "as of now your leave is canceled and your suspension of duty is lifted."

"Thank you, sir."

"When the officers arrive, I want you to tell them just what you told me."

Twenty-seven minutes later, Marcus had scrubbed himself clean with a rag and cold water, shaved, bandaged his wound, and was in uniform at the head of D Company. He was filling this position because Captain Forsyth was acting as battalion commander.

Marcus was shivering, though he didn't know if it was from the cold, or from excitement. This was to be a battle, not merely an encounter, nor even a skirmish of the type they had fought a few weeks earlier when the Indians escaped. This would be a planned attack on an enemy-held position. Such an operation, he knew, could only result in a full-scale, set-piece battle. It would be his first.

There was a great deal of activity going on right now. Men rode at a gallop through the snow from one end of the formation to the other to deliver messages or attend to last-minute details. Aside from the rustle of horses and the murmur of the men, the parade ground was quiet.

It was dark, but the white snow and the bright moon rendered the entire post visible. Marcus could see to the farthest end of the formation and he saw that the regiment was nearly in place. A few horses were still slipping into position, with clumps of snow dropping from their prancing hooves and clouds of vapor issuing from their nostrils.

On the porch of the sutler's store, all the women had gathered: officers' ladies and enlisted men's wives, along with the handful of unmarried women on the fort. Their dresses were covered now with coats, blankets, and robes as they fought the cold to watch their men depart on this strange, dangerous middle-of-the-night scout.

Finally, the clear, sharp notes of assembly played by the regimental trumpeter cut through the night air.

Now the shuffling around stopped, and the regiment grew quiet. Colonel Pettibone rode to the front of the formation, stood in his stirrups, and called to his battalion commanders.

"Form into line of march, column of fours, to the right."

The order of march given, the battalion commanders issued the commands and the regiment turned to the right.

"Guidons, post!"

Colonel Pettibone slapped his legs against the side of his horse, and it broke into a quick gallop to get him to the front of the formation. The regimental colors bearer rode with him, the colors snapping in the wind thus created.

Marcus was too far back to hear the marching order given, but he did hear Captain Forsyth issue the battalion command, and he passed it on to his company. He pulled his watch from his pocket and looked at it as they got under way. It was exactly thirty-three minutes from the time Colonel Pettibone dismissed the officers. From stand-down to mounted march in thirty-three minutes! He would have to write his tactics professor about that. It would be worth noting for the cadets who were just learning.

10

Marcus had been a cadet at West Point when Abraham Lincoln was killed. With other cadets, he had traveled to New York to take part in the great funeral parade, marching to the measured beat of the muffled drums. Memories of that sad occasion returned to him now as he rode through the harsh winter plains.

Although Colonel Pettibone had given orders that all loose equipment be tied down: sabers, canteens, cartridge belts, and the like, so that there would be no telltale jangle, that didn't mean that the movement was silent. In fact, quite the contrary was true, for the regiment's movement was accompanied by a continuous muffled beat as strong as the drumbeat had been on that sad day in New York, three and a half years before. But it wasn't the regimental drummer that provided the beat, though. It was the horses themselves, as their hooves broke through the hard crust of the day-old snow.

The colonel had given strict orders that no one was to speak above a whisper. There were to be no matches lit, nor pipes smoked, for even if the glow of pipes was concealed, the smell of tobacco could carry a great distance. Silently, for miles piling onto miles, the 4th Cavalry rode in the direction of Oushata.

Finally, as the regiment drew close to the place where Marcus and Missouri Joe had tied their horses when they sneaked into the village a couple of days earlier, a rider came back along the column, moving quickly. He stopped at the head of D Company and saluted Marcus.

"Colonel Pettibone's compliments, sir," the rider said. "And he asks that you join him at the head of the column."

"Lieutenant Culpepper, take command," Marcus ordered.

"Yes, sir," John answered.

Marcus rode back up along the column, following the messenger until he reached the head. There he saw Colonel Pettibone, Major Conklin, Captain Forsyth, and Missouri Joe.

"Lieutenant, we're going to halt the regiment here for a moment while a few of us ride ahead for a little scout. Since you were here before, I'd like you to come along with us."

"Yes, sir."

Leaving the regiment behind, Marcus rode along with Missouri Joe and the three senior officers until they reached the crest of a small hill, from which they could stare down on the village. All the tepees appeared to be tightly shut against the cold of the winter night. No one was moving anywhere.

"Good," Pettibone said, rubbing his hands together gleefully. "We've caught them completely by surprise. Major Conklin, how long will it take you to get your battalion around to the other side?"

"Forty-five minutes," Conklin replied.

"All right, say fifteen minutes to get back, and forty-five minutes for you to get into position. That means it will still be dark. We'll have that on our side."

"Colonel, what about women and children?" Forsyth asked. "By attacking while it is still dark, we'll be putting them at great risk." "Yes, I realize that," Pettibone said. "Unfortunately, we have no choice. Instruct your men to be particularly careful in selecting their targets. I don't want this to turn into another Sand Creek massacre. There are enough Indian lovers in Washington now. Such a massacre would only serve to unite them."

"Don't worry none about that, Colonel," Missouri Joe said, speaking up for the first time. "Iffen there's gonna be a massacre, I'm afraid it's gonna be the Indians doin' the killin'. They ain't no women or chillun in that there village."

Pettibone looked at Marcus with a questioning expression on his face. "Didn't you say you observed women, children, and old people in the village?"

"Yes, sir," Marcus answered. He was as surprised by Missouri Joe's statement as Pettibone was.

"Oh, yeah, they was some of 'em there when we was there," Missouri Joe said. "But they ain't none of 'em there now. They done left." "What makes you say that?"

"Look at that village, Colonel. They ain't a puff of smoke cornin' from any of the tepees. And listen, they ain't a baby cryin' or a dog barkin'."

"There are horses in the remuda," Forsyth pointed out.

"Not near enough horses for a village this size," Missouri Joe replied. "Just enough to make you think they's people there."

"What, exactly, are you getting at, mister?" Pettibone wanted to know.

"I figure when them Indians found the two men me an' the lieutenant kilt, they must've figured we was onto their village. They knowed we'd be a'comin' back, so they been waitin', an' now that we're here, they laid a trap for us. We're gonna attack a empty village, then they're gonna attack us. Now iffen you was to ask me, I think we ought to..." "Yes, well, thank you for your opinion," Pettibone interrupted. "But your job is only to lead us here. I'll make the tactical decisions." Pettibone took out his watch and looked at it. "Gentlemen, it is five of four. Set your watches accordingly. We will have a coordinated attack at exactly five o'clock. Listen for the call, that will be your signal to attack."

"Yes, sir," Conklin replied.

One hour later, Marcus was sitting on his horse, looking down at the quiet village below. He had seen nothing stirring down there from the moment they had moved into position.

Cavanaugh looked over at John Culpepper and saw the young lieutenant staring intently at the village below. It was bitterly cold and John's breath, like the breath of the others, was condensing into clouds of steam as he breathed. Marcus thought this scene would make a perfect picture for one of the dramatic woodcut scenes depicted in *Harper's Weekly*.

"Sergeant of the band," Pettibone called. Those were the first words spoken aloud since the troops had moved into position.

"Yes, sir," the bandmaster answered.

"It is nearly five o'clock. Prepare to play a march upon my signal."

"Yes, sir," the sergeant replied. He raised his baton and the band members lifted their instruments. When Pettibone brought his arm down, the band began to play and the soldiers of Forsyth's battalion let out a shout, then surged forward. They were quickly answered by shouts from Conklin's group on the other side, and the 4th began to close in on the village.

What had sounded like muffled drumbeats before, now sounded like the rolling thunder of timpani as the horses galloped across the wide-open field toward the village.

Conklin's battalion was much closer to the village, and therefore reached it first. Marcus heard them shooting and, at first, thought they were engaged. Then he realized that the shooting was all one sided and, even before they reached the edge of the village, Marcus saw Conklin's battalion riding through.

"Colonel Pettibone! The village is empty!" Forsyth shouted, and Pettibone held up his hand, halting the charge.

The men had been in the midst of a cavalry charge, and now they were brought to a rapid halt. They hauled back on the reins, and the horses, who had been committed to a full gallop, had difficulty in stopping. Some of them went on, a few of them even fell to their knees, while many more, confused by the conflicting instructions, turned and galloped off in a different direction.

What had been an organized cavalry attack suddenly turned into a disorganized and unstructured crowd of men and horse flesh. The continuity of command was broken and the greatest strength of a military unit, its order and discipline, was gone. As Marcus watched his own men galloping off in all directions, trying to regain control of their horses, he realized that it would probably take five minutes to reestablish the formation.

But they didn't have five minutes.

At the moment of the greatest confusion, they suddenly came under an immediate and exceptionally ferocious attack.

Cheyenne sprang up from behind rocks, fallen logs, and snow-covered embankments. There were hundreds of them, surely as many Indians as there were soldiers. And for the moment, at least, the advantage was fully with the Indians. They were fighting the battle exactly as they wanted to fight it. This wasn't a coordinated engagement with commanders issuing orders and maneuvering troops; this was five hundred individual battles with each participant, Indian and soldier, involved in his own personal fight.

Even though the Indians had no coordination of their efforts beyond the ambush, their positions were such that they were able to deliver a deadly crossfire upon the soldiers.

Marcus's horse was shot from under him, and he rolled through the snow, then stood up just as an Indian rushed him. The Indian was trying to claim coups with his war club, and Marcus leaned to one side, avoiding the first rush easily. When the Indian lost his footing in the snow and fell, Marcus shot him in the back of the head. The Indian's brains and blood scattered darkly onto the crest of the snow.

Suddenly a large soldier dismounted right in front of Marcus.

"Would you be takin' my horse, sir?" the soldier said.

"Sean O'Leary, are you crazy? Get back up on your horse!" Marcus ordered.

"Beggin' your pardon for disobeyin', but the men need a leader in the saddle," O'Leary said. Without waiting for a response, O'Leary physically picked Marcus up and set him on his horse, then slapped the horse's flanks, sending him forward. When Marcus got control of his horse and looked back toward O'Leary, he saw that the big man had just been hit with an arrow. The Indian who shot the arrow was no more than ten yards away, and as he tried to fit a second arrow into his bow, O'Leary charged him, then picked him up and broke the Indian's back across his knee like one would break a stick. Then O'Leary was hit with a bullet, and then another, before he fell, facedown, to lie motionless in the snow.

O'Leary wasn't the only one down. All around him, soldiers were being shot from their horses, then Marcus saw Pettibone's horse racing by with its saddle empty. Pettibone's foot was caught in the stirrup and he was being dragged behind the animal, though he knew nothing about it, because there was a bullet hole right in the middle of his forehead.

"Mr. Cavanaugh! Can you form a perimeter to our south?" Forsyth shouted.

"Yes, sir!" Marcus answered. He had no idea how he was going to do it, but he was grateful that someone had taken command in the field and there were some orders being issued.

Marcus saw John firing, taking carefully aimed shots, and he was gratified to see that despite the terror of the moment his friend was well in control of himself.

"Culpepper, take your platoon and form an anchor at that rock!" he ordered. "I'll complete the line! Dismount! Every fourth man, hold the horses."

With the two officers shouting instructions, D Company formed a defensive perimeter to the south.

With the perimeter established, Forsyth was able to regain control of the rest of the men, and the soldiers quit fighting their individual battles to fight as an organized army. The advantage passed from the Indians to the soldiers, and the Indians, realizing that, abandoned the field.

"They're getting away!" Marcus shouted to Forsyth.

"No, they're not, Marcus. Take your men after them!"

"Yes, sir!" Marcus replied happily. "D Company, get mounted and follow me!"

The horse handlers brought the mounts forward, and D Company leaped into the saddle. They thundered across the field after the Indians, and even though the Indians attempted to scatter in different directions, the pursuit was effective and many of them were killed.

Marcus recognized Two Eagles trying to make it to the edge of a wood line, but Marcus rode him down, knocking the Indian sprawling in the snow. He pulled his pistol and aimed it, knowing he could end it right here. For some reason he held back. He wasn't sure why, but he didn't pull the trigger. He had the idea that perhaps Two Eagles would be more valuable alive than dead.

Two Eagles jumped to his feet, holding his rifle in his hand. The rifle was packed solid with snow.

"Two Eagles. I am Cavanaugh," Marcus said.

"Cavanaugh!" Two Eagles grunted, and Marcus saw by the expression in Two Eagles's face that he knew who he was. "You die, Cavanaugh!" Two Eagles shouted.

"Marcus, look out!" John suddenly yelled, and Marcus looked around quickly to see that an Indian he had overlooked was aiming right at him. Marcus jerked back on the reins and his horse reared just as the Indian fired. The Indian's bullet missed. Marcus heard Two Eagles's rifle fire, then explode! He realized then that not only snow, but mud must've gotten down in the rifle barrel. The explosion tore away half of Two Eagles's face, killing him instantly.

The Indian who had fired at him and missed fired a second time, and Marcus whirled back toward him, just in time to see him going down with a bullet in his chest. He turned toward John, realizing John must have shot him, then let out a shout of despair.

"John! No!" he shouted.

Lieutenant Culpepper was on his knees, his hand on his stomach, blood spilling through his fingers. He and the Indian had shot each other at the same time.

"John!" Marcus shouted again, dismounting and running quickly to the side of his friend.

"What is it Shakespeare said?" John asked. "We owe God a death?" He tried to laugh, but the laughter turned into a cough. "I've always been one to pay my debts," he said.

John fell forward, lifeless, and Marcus held his head in his lap for a moment, then sadly stood up and looked around. The shooting was over now, and the predawn darkness had rolled away. The darkness had been replaced, however, by an early-morning fog which was growing thicker and which would soon limit visibility even more severely than had the darkness. It lent a ghostly atmosphere to the preceedings, and as Marcus watched, men and horses seemed to appear and disappear before his very eyes, moving as they did through the thickening morning mist.

By midmorning the fog had burned away and the soldiers moved through the abandoned village of Oushata with grim efficiency, burning the tepees and pulling down the lodges. The bodies of the slain soldiers had been collected and wrapped in ponchos, ready for the long trip back to the fort. Colonel Pettibone's body was among them ... so was Major Conklin, John Culpepper, Sean O'Leary, and Sergeant Flynn. In addition there were forty-six more, making a total of fifty-one officers and soldiers killed. Twenty- four had been wounded.

They had counted 112 Indians. The bodies of the slain Indians still lay in the snow, easily located by the bright red patterns of blood which marked their positions.

On the morning of the next day, carrying their wounded and dead with them on hastily constructed travois, the 4th Cavalry returned to Fort Reynolds. No word had been sent forward of their return, and their arrival wasn't known until they were sighted by the guards on the wall.

Martha Pettibone, Drusilla Conklin, and Janet Forsyth were gathered in Martha's parlor. Forsyth asked Marcus if he would accompany him when he took the tragic news to Pettibone and Conklin's wives.

"It's certainly not something I want to do," Marcus said. "Though I imagine it's something I'll be doing more than once in my career."

"Here are the men!" Janet said brightly the moment Marcus and Forsyth stepped into the room.

Marcus looked into Martha Pettibone's face and saw a little quizzical smile, as if she were asking what was detaining her husband. Then he looked into Drusilla Conklin's face and saw that there was no questioning look at all. Without being told, she knew the truth.

"My husband is not coming back, is he?" she asked in a quiet, pained voice.

"Oh, Drusilla, you poor thing," Martha said quickly. "As soon as Andrew gets in I'll . . ." Suddenly Martha realized, too, and she paused and looked back at Captain Forsyth and Marcus. She gasped and put her hand to her mouth.

"Oh, no," she said in a voice so small it might have come from a little girl. "Not Andrew, too?"

Neither Marcus nor Captain Forsyth had to answer, for the expression on their faces told all.

"How many?" Drusilla asked. "How many won't be coming back?"

"Fifty-one," Forsyth said.

"Who else? Your friend, Marcus? John Culpepper. Is he . . ."

Marcus shook his head sadly. "He was killed."

"What other husbands?" Drusilla asked. "Martha, we must go to the wives. We must see to them."

"Captain McPheeters, Lieutenant Varney, Sergeant Flynn," Forsyth said.

"Martha," Drusilla said.

Martha, whose face had gone chalk white, looked at Drusilla.

"Martha, we must go see the wives. They will need us."

"Yes," Martha said. "Yes, I ... I suppose they will. Yes, that's what Andrew would want me to do, isn't it?"

Martha and Drusilla left the commandant's quarters to call upon the widows of the other husbands who were killed. Marcus watched them, his admiration for Drusilla Conklin knowing no bounds.

"That's the bravest woman I ever saw," he said.

"Yes, she is," Janet agreed. "But then, one might say that she has had a head start on the others. You see, Major Conklin started killing himself a long time ago."

It was a month later when Marcus went into newly promoted Major Forsyth's office, to show him the latest issue of *Harper's Weekly*. The front cover of the magazine had a thrilling drawing of the battle between the 4th Cavalry and Two Eagles's Indians. The artist had used his imagination to the fullest, showing flying arrows, smashing war clubs, and slashing sabers. The illustration appeared carefully done—except for the sabers, of course.

"Pettibone's Last Fight," the caption read, and Colonel Pettibone was given the center-most position of the picture, using his right hand to drive a saber through an Indian's heart while, with the pistol in his left, he dispatched another, kicking away yet a third with his boot. All this with arrows already in his body.

"Well, Colonel Pettibone got all the glory he was hungering for," Marcus said, showing the paper to his commander.

Forsyth picked it up, looked at the picture, then opened it to read the story.

"Read the line where they say his leadership should be compared with the most gallant generals of the war?" Marcus asked.

Forsyth chuckled.

"I think someone should write that newspaper a letter and tell them the truth," Marcus said, obviously a little bitter about the story.

"And what is the truth, Marcus?" Major Forsyth asked.

"Well, for one thing, this business about his brilliant leadership. If he had listened to Missouri Joe, we wouldn't have blundered into that ambush in the first place. It was not a brilliantly planned battle, it was a riot. It wasn't until after Colonel Pettibone was already dead that you managed to rally the troops. And as for bravery, John Culpepper fought and died just as bravely as the colonel. Perhaps even more so."

"I see," Forsyth said, nodding gravely and walking toward the dark wooden sideboard.

He retrieved two glasses and a bottle of whiskey and poured two drinks.

"Marcus, as you stay in the Army longer, you'll learn that while the world may recognize a commander as hero, the true glory in battle belongs to his men. Any commanding officer worth his pay knows that. When you assume a command of your own, you'll understand how important it is."

"Thank you, sir . . . for the confidence in my future," Marcus said proudly.

"Well then, Cavanaugh," Major Forsyth said, raising his glass, "to future commands. . . ."

"And to duty and honor in the service of our country!"

GLOSSARY

- *Accoutrements.* Soldier's equipment, other than clothes or weapons.
- *Ambulance Wagon.* A four-wheeled, softly sprung, covered vehicle used to transport the wounded. In peacetime, it could be used as a coach.
- *Belly Robber.* A cook or cook's helper.
- *Bob Tail.* A soldier who has received a dishonorable discharge, so called because he would cut off the part of the document stating the type of discharge.
- *Brady.* Sometimes used to refer to a photograph, after Matthew Brady, the photographer.
- *Buffalo Gal.* A prostitute.
- *Buffalo Soldiers.* Black troopers with the 10th Cavalry, named by the Indians. The black

soldiers accepted the name proudly and made the buffalo their symbol.
- *Charioteers.* Cavalry term for wagon-riding infantrymen.
- *Coffee Cooler.* Loafer, one who shirks his duty.
- *Colors.* The Stars and Stripes, or the regimental flag.
- *Dog Robber.* Officer's orderly.
- E.M. Enlisted man, anyone who is not an officer.
- *Fiddlers' Green.* Old Army legend, which says that upon the death of any man who has ever heard the bugle or trumpet's wake-up call, he will go to neither heaven nor hell, but to a grassy glen under the shade trees, where he will drink whiskey and beer with all the other departed soldiers until reveille of Judgment Day.
- *French Leave.* Going absent without proper authority. Also called "going over the hill."
- *Garryowen.* The marching song of the 7 th Cavalry, still used by them today.
- *Goosewine.* Any type of brewed concoction used in place of coffee . . . such as grain or bark tea.
- *Heavies.* Slang term for anyone who was unable to ride, or ride well. Used by drill sergeants when addressing recruits.
- *Hooker.* Another term for prostitute, named

GLOSSARY

for the girls who followed General Hooker's army during the Civil War.
- *Hotchkiss Gun.* A breech-loading rapid-fire artillery piece which fires an explosive shell.
- *I.C. Brand.* Inspected and condemned (stamped on horses unfit for further duty). This was sometimes used as a way to tease old troopers.
- *In Garrison.* To remain on the post.
- *In Grade.* When a non-commissioned officer transfers from one company to another with the same rank.
- *Jenny Lind Steak.* Mule meat. In particular, a choice cut from upper lip of a mule.
- *Lister Bag.* A canvas bag used to hold drinking water. The evaporation of the water through the bag cools it.
- *Mule Skinner,* Mule Packer. Soldiers who work with the supply mules.
- *Noncom, NCO.* Non-commissioned officer. Corporals and sergeants are non-commissioned officers.
- *Officer.* A man who holds a commissioned rank by authority of the War Department, as granted by the United States Congress.
- *On Scout.* In the field.
- *Pup Tent.* Canvas field shelter. Each soldier carried half a tent in his pack. When two got together, they erected a small two-man tent.
- *Quadrangle.* The large square area, generally a

parade ground, around which the buildings of a fort are built. In the middle of the quadrangle is the flag and the signal cannon.
- *Remuda.* A small supply of horses confined by a hastily built stable, usually no more than a rope and hobble.
- *Shavetail.* A second lieutenant, so called because Army mules which were newly purchased had their tails shaved. The inference was that second lieutenants had no more sense than an untrained Army mule.
- *Sibley Stove. A* small, portable stove used for heating and cooking. It made a very efficient use of a small amount of wood.
- *Slum Burner. A cook.*
- Sutler's Store. Post provisioner under contract to the Army. Store served as a saloon and informal hall for celebrations as well. After 1869, the official name was the Trader's Store.
- *The Creature.* Alcoholic beverage.
- *Top-Knot.* Top of man's head or scalp.
- *Trader's Store.* After 1869, this was the more correct name for the sutler's stores, though old habits died hard, and many old soldiers referred to them as sutler's stores for many years afterward.
- *Uncle Sam's Watch and Chain.* The ball and chain used to restrain a prisoner.

- *Walking Draft.* A man with a price on his head.
- *Wind Jammer.* A bugler.

A LOOK AT CAVANAUGH'S ISLAND: BOOK 2 IN THE ARROW AND SABER SERIES

Fort Wallace, Colorado Territory: 1873

After reports of brutal Cheyenne attacks on small ranches, young Captain Marcus Cavanaugh and his men saddle up to intercept the renegade band. While they're gone, a grief-stricken settler takes matters into his own hands and ambushes an Indian camp, killing several braves.

Angered by the cowardly slaughter of his people, Chief Silver Bear vows revenge by enlisting the neighboring Sioux and Arapaho nations to declare war on the white man. When regular patrols can't stop the raiding parties, Captain Cavanaugh volunteers to take his company of Quick Riders to wipe out the hostiles and head off a full-scale uprising. But in a predawn attack, the three nations surround Cavanaugh's troops camped on a small island in the Arikaree River. Pinned down by enemy crossfire and low on supplies, they fight to hold their ground in the bloody battle for... CAVANAUGH'S ISLAND.

AVAILABLE OCTOBER 2018

ABOUT THE AUTHOR

Robert Vaughan sold his first book when he was 19. That was 57 years and nearly 500 books ago. He wrote the novelization for the miniseries *Andersonville*. Vaughan wrote, produced, and appeared in the History Channel documentary *Vietnam Homecoming*. His books have hit the NYT bestseller list seven times. He has won the Spur Award, the PORGIE Award (Best Paperback Original), the Western Fictioneers Lifetime Achievement Award, received the Readwest President's Award for Excellence in Western Fiction, is a member of the American Writers Hall of Fame and is a Pulitzer Prize nominee. Vaughn is also a retired army officer, helicopter pilot with three tours in Vietnam. And received the Distinguished Flying Cross, the Purple Heart, The Bronze Star with three oak leaf clusters, the Air Medal for valor with 35 oak leaf clusters, the Army Commendation Medal, the Meritorious Service Medal, and the Vietnamese Cross of Gallantry.

Made in the USA
Middletown, DE
19 December 2018